Praise for

THE

LEISURE
SEEKER

"One of the standards for a book is: Would I recommend it to friends? . . . I would recommend Michael Zadoorian's *The Leisure Seeker* to almost anyone." —*Detroit Free Press*

"I hoped for a book that would make me laugh during these tight times, and I was rewarded." —*Los Angeles Times*

"This is a purely character-driven novel, and Ella is a remarkable creation. . . . John is a distressingly realistic portrait of a person with Alzheimer's: Ella never knows when he'll have a moment of lucidity or fly into a dangerous rage. Her middle-aged children's panicked demands that the couple return home will resonate with any adult who has feared for a parent's well-being. . . . *The Leisure Seeker* is pretty much like life itself: joyous, painful, moving, tragic, mysterious, and not to be missed." —*Booklist* (starred review)

"Affecting. . . . An authentic and funny love story."
—*Publishers Weekly*

"Ella's final words on the page will haunt long after you close the book. Highly recommended." —*Route 66 News*

THE
LEISURE
SEEKER

MICHAEL ZADOORIAN is the author of the critically acclaimed novel *Second Hand* as well as the short story collection *The Lost Tiki Palaces of Detroit*. His fiction has appeared in *The Literary Review, Beloit Fiction Journal, Ararat, American Short Fiction, The North American Review*, and *Detroit Noir*. He lives with his wife in the Detroit area.

ALSO BY MICHAEL ZADOORIAN

Second Hand

THE
LEISURE
SEEKER

MICHAEL ZADOORIAN

HarperCollins*Publishers*

HarperCollins*Publishers* Ltd
1 London Bridge Street,
London SE1 9GF

www.harpercollins.co.uk

First published by HarperCollins*Publishers* 2009
This paperback edition published by HarperCollins*Publishers* 2018

1

A catalogue record for this book is available from the British Library

ISBN: 978-0-00-821219-3
Film tie-in ISBN: 978-0-00-828664-4

This novel is entirely a work of fiction.
The names, characters and incidents portrayed in it are
the work of the author's imagination. Any resemblance to
actual persons, living or dead, events or localities is
entirely coincidental.

Printed and bound in the UK by CPI Group (UK) Ltd, Croydon CR0 4YY

MIX
Paper from
responsible sources
FSC **FSC™ C007454**
www.fsc.org

This book is produced from independently certified FSC™ paper
to ensure responsible forest management.

For more information visit: www.harpercollins.co.uk/green

For Norm and Rose

Which is more fair,
The star of morning or the evening star?
The sunrise or the sunset of the heart?
The hour when we look forth to the unknown,
And the advancing day consumes the shadows,
Or that when all the landscape of our lives
Lies stretched behind us, and familiar places
Gleam in the distance, and sweet memories
Rise like a tender haze, and magnify
The objects we behold, that soon must vanish?
—HENRY WADSWORTH LONGFELLOW

The world is full of places to which I want to return.
—FORD MADOX FORD

One

MICHIGAN

We are tourists.

I have recently come to terms with this. My husband and I were never the kind who traveled to expand our minds. We traveled to have fun—Weeki Wachee, Gatlinburg, South of the Border, Lake George, Rock City, Wall Drug. We have seen swimming pigs and horses, a Russian palace covered with corn, young girls underwater drinking Pepsi-Cola from the seven-ounce bottle, London Bridge in the middle of a desert, a cycling cockatoo riding a tightrope.

I guess we always knew.

This, our last trip, was appropriately planned at the last minute, the luxury of the retiree. It is one that I'm glad I decided we take, although everybody (doctors, children) forbade us to go. "I strongly, strongly advise against any type of travel,

Ella," said Dr. Tomaszewski, one of the seemingly hundreds of physicians currently attending to me, when I hinted that my husband and I might take a trip. When I casually mentioned the idea of even a weekend getaway to my daughter, she used a tone that one would normally reserve for a disobedient puppy. (*"No!"*)

But John and I needed a vacation, more than we've ever needed one before. Besides, the doctors only want me to stay around so they can run their tests on me, poke me with their icy instruments, spot shadows inside of me. They've already done plenty of that. And while the children are only concerned with our well-being, it's still really none of their business. Durable power of attorney doesn't mean you get to run the whole show.

You yourself might ask: Is this the best idea? Two down-on-their-luck geezers, one with more health problems than a third world country, the other so senile that he doesn't even know what day it is—taking a cross-country road trip?

Don't be stupid. Of course it's not a good idea.

There's a story about how Mr. Ambrose Bierce, whose scary tales I enjoyed as a young girl, decided when he got to his seventies that he would simply shove off to Mexico. He wrote, "Naturally, it is possible, even probable, that I shall not return. These being strange countries, in which things happen." He also wrote: "It beats old age, disease, or falling down the cellar stairs." Speaking as someone who is acquainted with all three of those, I heartily agree with old Ambrose.

Put simply, we had nothing to lose. So I decided to take action. Our little Leisure Seeker camper van was packed and ready. We have kept it that way ever since retirement. So after assuring my children that a vacation was indeed out of the question, I kidnapped my husband, John, and we stole off, headed for Disneyland. That's where we took the kids, so we like it better than the other one. After all, at this point in our lives, we are more like children than ever. Especially John.

From the Detroit area, where we've lived all our lives, we make our way west across the state. It's a lovely trip so far, peaceful and steady. The air stream at my vent window creates a satin whoosh of white noise as the miles tug us from our old selves. Minds clear, aches diminish, worries evaporate, at least for a few hours. John doesn't speak at all but seems very content to drive. He's having one of his quiet days.

After about three hours, we stop for our first night in a small resort town that fancies itself an "artists' colony." As you enter the town proper, you pass, shrouded among the evergreens, a painter's palette the size of a children's wading pool, each daub of paint neatly dotted with a colored electric bulb that illuminates its corresponding hue. Next to it, a sign:

SAUGATUCK

This is where we spent our honeymoon almost sixty years ago (Mrs. Miller's Boarding House, long since burned down). We rode the Greyhound bus. That was our honeymoon: taking the dog to western Michigan. It was all we could afford, but it was exciting enough for us. (Ah, the advantages of being easily amused.)

After checking in at the trailer court, we two walk around town a bit, as much as I'm able, to enjoy what's left of the afternoon. I'm very pleased to be here again with my husband so many years later. It's been at least thirty years since we last visited. I'm surprised to find the town has not changed much—lots of confectioners, art galleries, ice cream parlors, and old-time shops. The park is where I remember it. Many of the early buildings are still standing and in good shape. I'm surprised that the town's fathers didn't feel the need to tear everything down and make it new. They must understand that when people are on vacation, they just want to return to a place that feels familiar, that still feels like it's theirs, even if just for a short time.

John and I sit on a bench on Main Street where the autumn air is heavy with the scent of warm fudge. We watch families pass by, wearing shorts and sweatshirts, eating ice cream cones, chattering away, their laughter low-pitched and lackadaisical, the unwound voices of people on vacation.

"This is nice," says John, his first words since we got here. "Is this home?"

"No, but it is nice," I say.

John is always asking if somewhere is home. Especially in the last year or so, when things started getting worse. The memory problems started about four years back, though there

4

were signs of it earlier. It's been a gradual process with him. (My problems arose much more recently.) I've been told that we're lucky, yet it doesn't feel that way. With his mind, first the corners of the blackboard were slowly erased, then the edges, and the edges of edges, creating a circle that grew smaller and smaller, before finally disappearing into itself. What is left are only smudges of recollection here and there, places where the eraser did not completely do its job, reminiscences that I hear again and again. Every once in a while, he knows enough to realize that he has forgotten much of our life together, but these moments happen less and less these days. It cheers me on the rare occasion when he is angered by his forgetfulness because it means he's still on this side, here with me. Most of the time, he's not. It's all right. I am the keeper of the memories.

During the night, John sleeps surprisingly well, but I hardly close my eyes. Instead, I stay up reading and watching some late-night talk-show nonsense on our tiny battery-powered TV. My only company is my wig up on its Styrofoam perch. We two sit here in the blue dim, listening to Jay Leno under the roar of John and his adenoids. It doesn't matter. I can't doze for more than a couple of hours, anyway, and it rarely affects me. These days, sleep feels like a luxury that I can scarcely afford.

John has left his wallet, coins, and keys on the table like he does at home. I pick up his massive sweat-cured leather brick of a billfold and open it. It gives off a mossy smell and makes a sticky noise as I flip through it. The wallet is a mess, the way I imagine his mind, things all mixed up and gummed together, tangled in the way I've seen in the brochures at the doctors' offices. In there, I find scraps of paper stained with illegible scrawl, calling cards from people long dead, an extra key for a car sold years ago, expired Aetna and Medicare cards next to new ones. I bet he hasn't cleaned it out in about a decade. I'm not sure how he manages to sit on the thing. No wonder his back always hurts.

I shove my fingers into one of the compartments and find a piece of paper folded twice over. Unlike everything else, it doesn't look like it's been there forever. I unfold it and see that it's a picture ripped from somewhere. At first glance, it seems to be a family photograph—people gathered together in front of a building, but none of the people in the photo are familiar to me. When I unfold the tattered fringe at the bottom, I see a caption:

FROM YOUR FRIENDS AT PUBLISHERS CLEARING HOUSE!

I should explain that we receive a ridiculous amount of mail from this company. At some point early in his illness, John fixated on the Publishers Clearing House company. He was always entering their sweepstakes, accidentally subscribing us to magazines that we didn't need—*Teen People*, *Off-Roader*, *Modern Ferret*. Pretty soon, those SOBs were sending us three letters every week. Later, it just got harder and harder for John to figure out the entry instructions, so the letters, opened and half-explored, started to pile up.

It takes me a moment, but I finally figure out why John has this picture in his wallet. He thinks it's a photo of his own family! I start laughing. I laugh so loud that I'm afraid that I'll wake him up. I laugh until tears come. Then I rip that photograph into a hundred tiny pieces.

Two

INDIANA

An early start through the gloom of interstate Indiana toward Chicago, where we will pick up Route 66 at its official starting point. Normally, we wouldn't go anywhere near a big city. They are dangerous places if you're old. You simply can't keep up and will be promptly ground into the pavement. (Remember that.) But it's Sunday morning and traffic is about as light as it gets. Even still, giant loud semitrucks grind and huff past us going 75, 80 mph and faster. Yet John is unshakable.

Though his mind is fading, he's still an excellent driver. I'm put in mind of Dustin Hoffman in that *Rain Man* movie. Maybe it's because of all our car trips in the past, or the fact that he's been driving since he was thirteen, but I don't think he'll ever forget how. Anyway, once you get into the rhythm of long-distance driving, it's only a matter of direction (my job—mistress of the maps), avoiding those sudden, unexpected exits, and looking out for the danger that comes up fast in your mirror.

Without notice, the air goes gray and flat. Foundries and factories shimmer in the distance, under a shroud of grimy haze.

John frowns, turns to me, and says, "Did you fart?"

"No," I say. "We're just going through Gary."

Three

ILLINOIS

Outside Chicago, the Dan Ryan Expressway isn't crowded, but everyone drives too damn fast. John tries to stay in the right lane, but lanes are continually added on or taken away. I'm sorry now we didn't just catch Route 66 out by Joliet, as I had originally planned. It's just that part of me needed to do this trip from the very beginning to the very, very end.

Unofficially, Route 66 starts right at Lake Michigan, at Jackson and Lake Shore Drive, which we find without much trouble. It's more difficult locating the official Route 66 starting point at Adams and Michigan. When we finally find the sign, I have John pull the van over. We could never do this on a workday, but this street is deserted today.

MICHAEL ZADOORIAN

BEGIN HISTORIC
ILLINOIS U.S. 66 ROUTE

I lean out the window to take a closer look, but I don't get out of the van. My wig could not survive this wind. It would be rolling down Adams like tumbleweed in a matter of seconds.

"This is it," I say to John.

"Yes sir," he says, with great enthusiasm. I'm not sure he understands what we're doing.

I direct us down Adams. We drive between buildings so tall that the sunlight can't reach us. This skyscraper twilight makes me feel strangely safe. Once we get onto Ogden Avenue, I start to see Route 66 signs.

In Berwyn, there are Route 66 banners hanging from the lampposts. I spot a place called Route 66 Realty. When we get to Cicero, Al Capone's old stomping grounds, everyone just seems to be waking up. Folks are out driving around, but in no hurry, taking their Sunday morning time.

I realize that if John and I want to survive this trip, we must behave the same way. No rushing, no pressure, no four-lane superhighways if we can help it. There were too many vacations like that with the kids. Two days to get to Florida, three to California—*we've only got two weeks*—rush, rush, rush. Now there's all the time in the world. Except I'm falling apart and John can barely remember his name. But that's all right. I remember it. Between the two of us, we are one whole person.

Along the side of the road, two small children fresh from church wave to us. John honks the horn. I hold my hand up and wave at the wrist like I'm Queen Elizabeth.

We pass a statue of an enormous white chicken.

Did you know that there are parts of Route 66 that are buried directly beneath the freeway? It's true. They paved right over it, the heartless bastards. That's why Route 66 is a dead road today, decommissioned, emblems torn off its shoulders like a disgraced soldier.

When we reach one of these freeway stretches, John naturally accelerates, an instinct bred in the lead foot of a Detroit boy.

"Goose it, John!" I say, feeling freer than I have in years.

From our lofty vantage in the Leisure Seeker, the entombed Route 66 flies beneath us with a billowy roar. Suddenly sleepy, I crack the window, releasing a vacuum rush of balmy air, a sound like the flick of a newly laundered top sheet. I want the wind in my face. In the glove box, I find a fold-up plastic babushka, an ancient giveaway from a dry cleaner in our old neighborhood in Detroit. I wrap it around my wig, tie it under my chin, then roll down the window. The bonnet bellows out like it's going to launch off my head, wig and all. I roll the window back up most of the way.

Morning is well established now, the weather quite perfect. A brilliant September day, that gaudy Crayola Yellow sunny, like you find at the uppermost corner of a child's drawing. Yet

I can still detect the breath of fall in the air, damp-dry and musky. It's the kind of autumn day that used to make me feel as if anything was possible. I remember a road trip years back, when the kids were still with us, looking out over the plains of Missouri on a day like this and feeling for a moment that life could continue indefinitely, that it would never end.

Strange what a little sunshine can make you believe.

These days, autumn is no longer my favorite season. Dead, shriveled leaves don't hold quite the appeal they used to. I can't imagine why.

The layer-cake freeway ends and we're back on Route 66. I can tell by the giant green-suited spaceman standing alongside the road.

"John, look!" I say, as we approach the emerald colossus, his massive noggin in a fishbowl helmet.

"How about that?" says John, eyes barely straying from the road. He couldn't care less.

As we pass the Launching Pad Drive-In, again I want to crank down the window all the way. Then I realize that if I want to feel the wind and sun on my face, there is no reason why I can't. I rip off my babushka, then unclasp my helmet of synthetic lifelike fiber (the Eva Gabor Milady II Evening Shade—75% white/25% black) at the back where it is tentatively tethered to my last remaining hair of any thickness. I reach underneath, then pull back and up to unsheathe my head.

I roll down the window and throw that goddamned thing out where it tumbles and flops along the side of the road like a just-hit animal. Such blessed relief. I can't remember the last time my scalp saw direct sunlight. What little hair I have on top is thin and delicate like the first frail wisps of an infant. In the delicious wind, the long strands twist and dance around my scalp, a sad swirled turban, but I don't care today. It had bothered me so much when my hair thinned out after menopause. I was ashamed like I had done something wrong, afraid of what everyone would say. You spend your life so worried about what others think, when in reality, people mostly don't think. On the few occasions when they do, true, it is often something bad, but one has to at least admire the fact that they're thinking at all.

I look back at my Styrofoam wig stand. The head is still taped to the counter, no longer my companion, but now staring at me, judging, wondering "What the hell did you just do?" I don't look at myself in the mirror. I know I look like death warmed over. It doesn't matter. I feel lighter already.

Up ahead, I spot a building that looks somehow familiar. Low slung and sprawling, its peaked turquoise roof is blanched from decades of sun. There's a faded horse and carriage on the side of the building. Finally, I notice the sign.

STUCKEY'S

On our vacations with the kids, Kevin and Cindy, we'd often stop at those places with their pecan logs and acrid coffee. Sometimes the signs would start a hundred miles away.

There'd be a new one every ten, fifteen miles. The kids would get all worked up and want to stop and John would say no, we had to get some miles under our belt. They'd beg and finally when we were a half mile away, he'd give in. The kids would scream *yay*, and John and I would smile at each other like parents who knew how to spoil their children just enough.

A semitruck roars past us. In a moment, it's silent again, except for the wind. "I haven't seen one of those places in years," I say. "Do you remember Stuckey's, John?"

"Oh yeah," he says, in a tone that almost makes me believe him.

"Come on," I say. "Let's go. We need gas anyway."

Nodding, John pulls up to the pumps. No sooner do I get out of the van than a man, neatly dressed in a beige sport shirt and copper-colored slacks, approaches us.

"We don't have gas anymore, but there's a BP up the road," he says, his voice raspy, but not unpleasant. He tips his puffy white cap back on his head with his thumb.

"It's okay," I say. "We really just wanted a pecan log."

He shakes his head. "We don't have those anymore, either. We're just gone out of business."

"Oh, I'm sorry to hear that," I say, clutching my armrest. "We used to like Stuckey's. We came with our kids."

He shrugs forlornly. "Everyone did."

As he walks away, I wrestle myself back into the van. By the time I'm buckled up and ready to give John the go-ahead, the man is back at my door.

"I found one," he says, handing me a pecan log.

He's gone before I can even thank him.

I find out now that Route 66 was already starting to fall apart the time we traveled on it in the '60s. Much of the old road is closed now, buried or bulldozed, long ago replaced by Highways 55 and 44 and 40. In some places, the original pink Portland concrete is so decrepit you can't even drive on it. Yet there are maps and books available now that show the old route, turn-by-turn directions, guides to the trailer parks. It's true. I found it all on the World Wide Web in the library. Turns out people didn't want to let go of the old road, that a lot of the kids who were born after the war, who traveled it with their parents, want to retrace their steps. Apparently, everything old is new again.

Except us.

"I'm hungry," says John. "Let's go to McDonald's."

"You always want to go to McDonald's," I say, poking his arm with the pecan log. "Here. Eat this."

He looks at it with suspicion. "I want a hamburger."

I stash the pecan log in our snack bag. "We'll find you a hamburger somewhere else for a change."

John loves McDonald's. I'm not that crazy about it, but he could eat it every day. He did for quite some time. McDonald's was his hangout for a number of years after he retired. Every day, Monday through Friday, right around midmorning. After a while, I started to wonder what the big attraction was, so I went with him. It was just a bunch of old farts sitting around, chewing the fat, drinking Senior Discount coffees, reading the paper and bitching about the state of the world. Then they'd get a free refill and start all over again when new old farts arrived. I couldn't get out of there fast enough. I never went with him again, which I think was what he wanted. Frankly, I think John just needed somewhere to go to get away from me after he retired. Truth be told, I was happy to have him out of my hair, synthetic or otherwise.

Yet once we both settled into the rhythm of retirement, we had a good time. We were both in pretty decent shape then, so we did a lot. After John would return from McDonald's, we'd take care of things around the house, run errands, chase down the sales at the supermarkets or Big Lots, catch a matinee, have an early dinner. We'd gas up the Leisure Seeker and take off for weekends with friends or take the long trek to the outlet mall at Birch Run. It was a good period, one that didn't last long enough. Soon, we started spending our days going from doctor's office to doctor's office, our weeks worrying about tests, our months recovering from procedures. After a while, just staying alive becomes a full-time job. No wonder we need a vacation.

We manage to avoid McDonald's long enough to stop for lunch somewhere outside Normal, Illinois. I grab my four-pronged cane and lower myself from the van. John, still pretty spry, has already gotten out on his side to help me. "I got you," he says.

"Thanks, honey."

Between the two of us, we do all right.

Inside, the diner is meant to look like the 1950s, but it doesn't look anything like how I remember them. Somewhere along the line, people became convinced that that decade was all about sock hops, poodle skirts, rock and roll, shiny red T-birds, James Dean, Marilyn Monroe. and Elvis. It's funny how a whole decade gets reduced into a few seemingly random pictures. For me, that decade was about diapers and training wheels and miscarriages and trying to house and feed three people on $47 a week.

After John and I sit down at a table, a girl dressed as a carhop walks up. (Why a carhop? We're *inside,* for Christ's sake.) She has long bottle-blond hair, bow lips, and eyes like a kewpie doll.

"Welcome to the Route 66 Diner," she says, in a whispery voice. "I'm Chantal. I'll be your server."

I don't know what to say to this, so I just say something. "Hello, Chantal. I'm Ella and this is my husband, John. I guess we'll be your customers."

"I want a hamburger," says John, abruptly. He's lost a few of his social skills along with the memory.

I try to laugh it off. "We'll both have plain hamburgers and coffee," I say.

Chantal looks disappointed. Maybe she works on commission. "How about some Fabian Fries? A Pelvis Shake?"

"What is *that*?"

"A chocolate milk shake." She gives me a little nod. "They're good."

"All right. You don't have to twist my arm."

"Pelvis Shake, coming right up," she says, pleased to have made a sale.

After our new friend Chantal leaves, I excuse myself to make a phone call.

"Mom, where the fuck are you?" screams my daughter over the phone, right there in the lobby of the diner.

I look around, almost embarrassed to be listening to her. I don't know where she got this mouth, but it wasn't from me, I assure you.

"Cindy honey, don't use that language. Your father and I are fine. We're just taking a little trip."

"I can't believe you went through with this. We all discussed this and decided that you and Dad taking any kind of a trip was out of the question."

I can hear the exasperation in her voice. I don't like it when Cindy gets all worked up. She's been having blood pressure problems lately, and getting all frantic certainly doesn't help.

"Cindy. *Calm down*. Your father and I didn't decide anything. You and Kevin and the doctors decided for us. Then, Dad and I decided that we should go anyway."

"Mom. You're sick."

"Sick is relative, dear. I'm way past sick."

"I can't believe you're doing this," she says, indignantly. "You can't just stop going to the doctor."

I look around the restaurant to make sure no one is listening. I lower my voice. "Cynthia, I am not going to let them do their treatments on me."

"They just want to try to make you better."

"How? By killing me? I'd rather go on vacation with your father."

"Damn it, Mom!"

"I *don't* like being yelled at, young lady."

There is a long pause while Cindy gives herself a time-out. She used to do this when she was frustrated with her kids, now she does it with John and I.

"Mother," she says, newly composed. "You know Dad shouldn't even be driving in his condition."

"Your father still drives just fine. I wouldn't go with him if I didn't think that."

"What if you guys get in an accident because of him? What if he hurts someone?"

I know she has a point, but I also know John. "He's not going to hurt anyone. If they let sixteen-year-olds on the road to run wild, then your father, who has an excellent driving record, should be able to do the same."

"Oh God. *Mother*," she says, her voice rising, signaling surrender, "where are you?"

"It doesn't matter. We just stopped for lunch."

"Where are you going?"

I don't appreciate the "20 Questions" from my daughter.

I'm not even sure I should tell her, but I do anyway. "We're going to go to Disneyland."

"*Disneyland?* In California? You cannot be serious." This is where I realize that my daughter still has the flair for the dramatic that she developed when she was a snotty teenager.

"Oh, we're serious." I think I'm going to end this call soon. Who knows? They could be putting a tracer on the call, like on the television.

"Oh God. I can't believe this. Do you at least have the cell phone we bought you?"

"I do, but I don't like that thing, honey. But I've got it in case of an emergency."

"Would you please at least turn it on," she says, pleading, "so I can keep in touch with you?"

"I don't think so. Don't worry so much. Your father and I will be fine. It's just a little vacation."

"Mom—"

"Love you, honey." It's time to hang up, so I do. She'll be fine, but she's crazy if she thinks I'm going to turn on that cellular telephone. I've got more than enough cancer, thank you.

Back at the table, John and I eat our Route 66 burgers. My chocolate Pelvis Shake is not half bad.

Back on the road, the fatigue comes on hard and sudden. I want to tell John to call it a day, but we've only been driving for about four hours. I try to ignore it. After the phone

22

call with Cindy, I want to put more distance between us and home. Yesterday I was afraid to leave home for all the obvious reasons, but now that we are gone, I want us to be *really* gone.

John turns to me, looking concerned. "Are you all right, miss?"

"Yes, I am, John." He is having one of his moments where he knows I am someone dear to him, but he's not entirely sure who I am.

"John. Do you know who I am?"

"Of course I do."

"Then who am I?"

"Oh, knock it off."

I put my hand on his arm. "John. Tell me who I am."

He stares at the road, looking annoyed, but worried. "You're my wife."

"Good. What's my name?"

"For Christ's sake," he says, but he's thinking. "It's Ella," he says, after a moment.

"That's right."

He smiles at me. I put my hand on his knee, give it a squeeze. "Keep your eyes on the road," I say.

As far as what John does and does not remember, I cannot say. He does know who I am most of the time, but then we have been together so long that even if he is slowly working his way back in time, forgetting as he goes, I'm still there with him. I wonder: are the eyes deceived along with the mind? If it is, say, 1973 to him, do I look as I did back then? And if I don't (which I most certainly don't), how does he know it's me? Does that make sense?

Route 66 is the frontage road of I-55 for this stretch. To the left of us, telephone poles, blackened with age and exhaust and crowned with blue-green glass insulators (the kind you sometimes see in antique shops), run parallel to the highway. Some of the poles are broken and splintered, toppled or teetering over in some places, the lines long snapped and dangling; yet many still retain their wires, and they somehow connect us to the road like an old streetcar, as if we are tethered to the air.

On the other side: the freeway and the railroad tracks that will follow the road pretty much all the way to California. Between our road and the freeway, I see barricaded patches of what must be a very old alignment of 66, a narrow pinkish path that barely looks wide enough for one car. Nature is slowly reclaiming it. Vegetation creeps in from the edges, narrowing it like an artery. Weeds grow in the crevices roughly every six feet or so, where the slabs were poured. In a few more years, you won't even be able to see this old highway.

When we're not on the frontage road, we pass through tiny, desperate towns. Once everyone stopped taking Route 66, there was no reason for anyone to stop and spend money in these places, so they just languished. In one burg called Atlanta, we pass another fiberglass giant (as they refer to them in my guidebook). This one is Paul Bunyan holding a gigantic frankfurter.

"Well, look at that," says John. It's the first one he's shown any interest in.

"They just moved it here from Chicago."

"What for?" he says.

I look around this street, all boarded up and joyless. "That, my dear, is the sixty-four-thousand-dollar question."

We pull over, roll down our windows to look up at the giant's bulging forearms. According to my guidebook, he was originally holding a muffler, so now the wiener sits on the top of a clawed left hand withered shut. It looks like Bob Dole holding a jumbo hot dog. It makes me sad to think of these people pinning all their hopes on this thing to bring their little ghost town back to life.

Outside Springfield, we stop for the night. The park is not so much a campground, but a trailer village, with a few extra spaces that they rent out to folks with campers. Basically, it's like camping in the middle of someone's crummy neighborhood. But we were tired and it was available.

We settle in, hook up our electricity, water, and septic lines. (Between what John remembers and what I remember him teaching me, we muddle through the various plugs and connections.) We have sandwiches and take our meds, then John lies down for a snooze. I let him sleep because it feels good to be by myself sitting at the picnic table.

Next door, our neighbors arrive home for the night. First

the man of the house arrives in a beat-up Olds, the hood and roof covered with a vast landscape of rust, a corroded map of the world. When I wave hello, he stares right through me and heads inside the trailer. Minutes later, the woman shows up on foot. Still in her Wal-Mart smock, she's tanned and rail thin—that kind of beef jerky look that I associate with either two-pack-a-day smokers or those people who run long-distance races. When I wave to her, she marches right over.

"Hey, neighbor!"

I smile at her. "Just for the evening, I'm afraid."

"I'm Sandy," she says, holding out her hand.

"Ella," I say, shaking it.

She lights a butt, then launches right into it. "Lord, what a day I've had. My manager was on my ass from the moment I punched in till the moment I walked out of there. He searched me out while I was eating my lunch, I swear it! I was sitting there, nice as you please, eating my Salisbury steak when he comes up to me and starts giving me grief about the inventory we've got coming up. He's screaming at me during lunch! Can you imagine? I just sat there and shoveled food into my mouth right in front of him. And I didn't close it, either. I just left it wide open and chewed while he bitched away. I even let a little fall from my mouth onto my plate. He didn't even notice. I figured, hell, I'm on my lunch hour and I'm gonna eat my lunch whether he likes it or not . . ."

This goes on for quite some time. Smoking and talking. Talking and smoking. She just lights one off the other. I feel sorry for her at first, that she needs to do this with complete strangers, but after about twenty minutes, I was afraid that I was going to be out there all night. Poor thing, I know she just wanted to make a noise, have someone to pay attention to her, know she was there. She didn't understand that it didn't matter that I knew she was there. I would be gone tomorrow. You need to have it matter to people who count.

"My first husband, he gave me gonorrhea for our fourth anniversary. He was a sonofabitch, that one. He about wore me out with his hijinks—"

Right then, her husband comes out, and without a word, grabs her arm and starts pulling her back to their little place.

"Ow! Donald! What are you doing?"

He didn't say a word, but she chattered and smoked all the way there. After the door shut, I could still hear her talking.

Twilight slips in like a timid creature. Lights tick on around the trailer village. The air grows cooler. I grab one of John's old jackets and throw it over my shoulders. In a storage bin, I find an old gray wool winter cap to put on my head, which is freezing, unaccustomed to being without its hat of hair. The cold and the musky smell of John's jacket make me think of a night after we were first married in the winter of 1950. We were living on Twelfth Street just off West Grand Boulevard. It had rained all night as the temperature plummeted. At about midnight, it stopped, and John and I, for some reason, decided to take a walk.

It was frigid, but so beautiful. Everything was coated with

a thick layer of brilliant clear ice, as if the world were preserved under glass. We had to take tiny hesitant steps, so as not to slip. Above us, power lines crackled and tore from their poles; a streetlight globe, laden with ice, dropped and shattered in the street with a muffled *pop*. We walked and walked under a brittle black sky, jagged with stars, moon shining hard and bright on the crystal buildings that lined the boulevard. The world looked fragile, but we were young and invulnerable. We kept walking, at least a mile, toward the golden tower of the Fisher Building, not knowing why, knowing only that we needed to get there. We returned to our flat that night excited, our hair glistening with shiny flecks of ice, full of a deep thirst for each other. That was the night that Cindy was conceived.

Right now, I hear the loudening trill of crickets and the sizzle of gravel as cars slowly pass. I can smell microwave popcorn coming from somewhere. There is no reason to, but I feel safe with all these people around us. John is awake now and I can hear him talking under his breath. He is telling someone off. I hear him whispering obscenities, threats to enemies, accusations. All our lives together, John was a passive, quiet man. But now, since he started to lose his mind, he says the things that he always wanted to say to people. He is forever reading his personal riot act to someone. It often happens this time of the day. When the sun sets, the anger rises in him.

He appears at the doorway of the van. "Where are we?" he says loud, voice full of fight.

"We're in Illinois," I say, ready for it.

"Is that home?"

28

"No. Home is Michigan."

"What are we doing here?" he barks.

"We're on vacation."

"We are?"

"Yes. And we're having a great time."

He crosses his arms. "No, I'm not. I want a cup of tea."

"I'll make one in a little while. I'm resting."

He joins me at the table. It's quiet for about a minute, then he speaks again. "How about a cup of tea?"

"We're going to wait a little while for a cup of tea."

"Why?"

"Because you'll be up all night peeing."

"Goddamn it, I want a cup of tea!"

Finally, I give him a look and talk to him in that same hushed, threatening voice he was using a minute ago. "Keep your voice down. People live around here. Why don't you get up and make it yourself? You're not crippled."

"Maybe I will."

He won't. I don't think he really knows where anything is in the camper anymore. He just sits there stewing. This is the price I pay for him being sweet as pie all day long. Maybe it was just that he had something to do. We never usually drive this much. It seems to help when he has something to occupy him.

"How about a cup of tea?" John says, like it's a new idea that came to him just this second.

"All right," I say.

I get up and make us both a cup of tea.

It's night and John is miraculously sleeping again. I, of course, can't doze off to save my life. I'm not used to the camper yet, how closed in it is, like some rolling tan-and-brown striped recreational sarcophagus. The Leisure Seeker really is quite small. At the moment, I'm just across from the side rear door, sitting in our social area. It's a little Formica table with a plaid cushioned bench on either side. This is where we eat or play cards (or sometimes sleep if you're me). Across from here is my kitchen with a three-burner stove (which I never use), a tiny radar range, a sink about the size of a dishpan, and a little fridge. The bed where John is sleeping is at the very back just under the rear window. It's a couch that folds out to a double bed. The world's smallest bathroom is right nearby, which is helpful when you get up as much as we do in the middle of the night. There's another sleeping space above the driver's compartment that hasn't been used in years, as well as various closets, storage spaces, and cubbyholes. At the very front are the captain's chairs, big overstuffed adjustable seats for the driver and the passenger. They're by far the most comfortable seats in the house.

We got the Leisure Seeker a long time ago, so while the decor isn't exactly current, it's still pretty. It's done in earth tones—wood-grain paneling; harvest gold and avocado green curtains; nubby gold, green, and brown plaid upholstery, all still in beautiful Scotchgarded condition. We take care of our things.

I know some people don't consider what we do to be camping, and I suppose it's not particularly rustic, but I've always found it to be a happy medium between hotels and really roughing it. The only reason we ever really started was to save money. We had a little Apache pop-up camper that we hauled around for quite a few years. We could camp for about two dollars a night. It was cheap and fun and I always thought that the kids loved it. But neither Kevin nor Cindy camp now. They tell me now that when they were kids, they would have much preferred to stay in motels with pools and TV and restaurants. Oh well, tough titty.

I pull myself up from the table, open the side door, step outside, and listen to the night. It's quiet now and I can hear the semitrucks highballing down the freeway in the distance. That sound makes me yearn for something, but I don't exactly know what. I used to find it soothing back when we had a camperful and would pull over to some trailer park next to a freeway, bone tired, but pleased over how much distance we'd covered.

I decide that maybe a drink would help me get to sleep. I drag out the bottle of Canadian Club that I made sure we packed, and I mix myself a little highball with some 7UP. It goes without saying that I'm not supposed to drink, but hell, I'm on vacation. I settle back down at the table with my drink, listen to the faraway grind of the trucks, and start to feel more comfortable right away.

I wake up at 6:40 with a headache and a bladderful. After I visit the bathroom, I fill our electric kettle and plug it in. Outside, it's just getting light. I hear chickadees chattering over the sound of car doors slamming shut. John, still in bed, is a little restless. When he opens his eyes, he turns to me and speaks in a surprisingly matter-of-fact voice, as if resuming a conversation we started last night. It is the old John, come to visit.

"Haven't slept in the camper for a while, have we? Feels pretty good. How'd you sleep, hon?"

I walk over to the bed, sit on the ledge next to it. "Not great. But it is nice to be camping again, isn't it?"

"Sure is. Where are we again?" He rubs his cheeks and pulls at his bottom lip.

He's like this in the mornings sometimes, normal as can be. "We're in Illinois," I say. "About a hundred miles from the Missouri state line."

"Wow. We're making good time, aren't we?"

"Uh-huh."

"Boy, it feels good to be on the road again. Feels right."

"Yes, it does."

The ridges in his forehead ripple and furrow. "Have you talked to the kids?"

"I spoke to Cindy yesterday at lunch. She's worried about us being on vacation."

"Why's she worried?" He gets up, arches his back to get the kinks out. "Uggh," he groans. "Old man Mose."

"Oh, you know Cindy. She's a worrier."

He smiles at me. "I wonder where she got that from."

I smile back, wrangle myself off the ledge, and kiss him good morning. I touch the ruddy mottled skin of his head, smooth back the wisps of dampish gray hair on both sides of that endless forehead. On these days, morning is like a return, a meeting up again.

"Hey, is there water on for coffee?" I nod, then head back over to the counter and pour us both a cup of instant. I stir in a half packet of Sweet'n Low in his mug and take it over to him. He has lain down again, closed his eyes.

"John?"

He opens them and looks at me. "Where are we?"

"I just told you, honey. We're in Illinois."

"No, you didn't."

"Yes, I did, John."

"Is this home?"

And just like that, the old John is gone. This is how it happens. Sometimes I get him for a few minutes in the morning, wonderful moments when he actually acts like himself, as if his mind has forgotten to be forgetful. Then suddenly it's like our whole conversation never happened. I should get used to this, but I just can't.

"Why don't you get dressed, John? And put some clean clothes on."

"All right."

I step outside and sit on a lawn chair to take my meds.

This morning, I seem to be in some "discomfort," as my doctors love to call it, so I take one of my little blue oxycodone pills along with the fistful of meds I usually take. I don't really want to cloud my judgment since I'm the commander of this ship of fools, but it's quite a bit of discomfort, take my word for it.

I hear John inside the trailer, getting dressed. He could probably use some help, but I don't want to talk to him for a while. I want to enjoy those few lucid minutes with him while they're still fresh in my memory.

Soon, we're as cleaned up as either of us are going to get. John is wearing a loud green plaid shirt and beige plaid pants. I almost tell him that it looks like he belongs at the Barnum & Bailey circus, but these days I'm just happy to get him into clean clothes. Who am I to talk, anyway? I've replaced my wig with Kevin's old wool baseball cap, one that he used to wear constantly when he went camping with us. I almost put it on backward like I see the kids do, but then I change my mind. There are degrees of foolishness, after all. Maybe later I'll make do with a babushka, but for now I love this old Detroit Tigers cap.

Back on 66, John is in good spirits, not like he was this morning, but cheery and driving well. As for me, I feel both the caffeine and the drugs work their magic on me. My fingertips tingle. My heart whirrs like a thrush. I am alert, euphoric just to be traveling. The thrum of our tires on the pavement is joyous music to me, quelling my fears, transiting my discomfort to a place far up the road, a shuddering speck on the apparent horizon.

Here now, we have entered another state.

Four

MISSOURI

We pass a church with a massive blue neon cross, and I am spiritually lifted by feelings of great religiosity. No, I'm not, for crying out loud. Don't be ridiculous. But what I do love about this road is how the gaudy becomes grand, how tastelessness is a way of everyday life. You have to admire how these people shamelessly try to get your attention as you drive by, whether they're trying to feed you a hamburger or a savior.

We merge onto I-270, so to bypass St. Louis. We cross the Mississippi on a long, pocked suspension bridge that's older than either of us. The dirty water roils beneath, licks up at us like liquid earth. I'm relieved when I see the sign:

WELCOME TO MISSOURI

Old as I am, I still get a thrill from that. Yet after this brief pleasure, some schnook in a big blue SUV, the kind everyone drives nowadays, cuts us off.

"John! Watch out!" I cry, sure that we're going to smash into his rear end. I crush my foot to the floorboard, squeeze my eyes shut, and wait for the impact.

John slams on the brakes and veers right. I jerk forward; my seat belt locks tight against my chest. Sunglasses and guidebooks fly from the seats. I hear a cupboard snap open in the back and canned goods hammer the floor. I open my eyes to find John staring absently at the taillights of the oblivious driver ahead. "We're all right," he mutters.

I told you, John is an excellent driver.

A few miles later, we come up behind the big blue truck again when it has to slow for traffic. When he hits the brakes, I see that someone has written something in the dust on his back window, directly on the third taillight they put on the new cars. When he hits the brakes again, the words flash at us:

DRIVEN BY DICKHEAD

After we finish laughing, we make it back onto 66.

Every once in a while, I see something that looks like it's from the old days of the highway—a sun-scorched streamline filling station or chalky ramshackle motor court with a half-lit

VACANCY sign. More often than not, though, there are only ruins, or simply a faded and rusted sign off the road in front of an empty field. They conjure up strange, random memories for me—the few dusty, deafening, rattletrap journeys I took with my parents ages ago to leaden towns like Lansing, Michigan, or Cambridge, Ohio. (There were no vacations back then, only purposeful visits to sullen relatives, always for deaths or the unhappy work that followed them.)

The sad truth is, John and I and the kids only took Route 66 once on our trips to Disneyland. Our family, like the rest of America, succumbed to the lure of faster highways, more direct routes, higher speed limits. We forgot about taking the slow way. It makes you wonder if something inside us knows that our lives are going to pass faster than we could ever realize. So we run around like chickens about to lose our heads.

Which makes our little two- or three-week vacations with our families more important than ever. I remember so much about our trips together: the tap of moths around a Coleman lantern as we played cards at a picnic table; constructing olive loaf sandwiches on the top of a cooler while John drove us through a Colorado spring snowstorm; reading the Arizona newspapers by brilliant moonlight on the shores of Lake Powell; stashing comic books in the trunk of our old Pontiac for Kevin, doling them out one at a time to keep down the whining and boredom; the cool gray formations of the South Dakota Badlands, rising from the earth like stone mammoths; eating chuck wagon barbecue in a giant teepee in Jenny Lake, Wyoming; the chugging penny slots at the old

Vegas Stardust; and so many more I can't even describe. As for the time that elapsed between those vacations, that's another thing altogether. It seems to have all passed breathlessly, like some extended whisper of days, months, years, decades.

At Stanton, I direct John into the parking lot of Meramec Caverns. Ever since we started this trip, we've been seeing signs for the place everywhere—billboards, roofs, bumper stickers, on the sides of barns.

"Come on, John, you want to go see the caverns?"

"What for?" he says, in a tone that I don't care for.

I forget that I can't really ask his opinion anymore because if he's in one of his contrary moods, he will argue with me about whether water is wet. I have to remember what the doctors have told me, to not ask him, but to tell him.

"Here we are," I say, as we park near a statue of Frank and Jesse James. Apparently, those James boys hid out here for a while. As a fellow fugitive, I feel right at home. I grab my trusty cane and we head on in.

Yet as soon as we try to purchase our tickets, we have problems. The young man behind the ticket desk gives me the once-over. He's a red-faced little turd with a fake ranger uniform that's two sizes too big for him.

"Ma'am, the tour is kinda long. I think you're gonna need, like, a wheelchair," he says.

"I most certainly do not," I say.

He makes a face like he just tasted something bad. "The

tour's like about a mile and a half. Some of it's uphill, and the walkways are wet a lot. We've had people, like, fall. It's really, really hard to get a stretcher in there."

I look over at John. He shrugs, no help at all.

"Fine," I snap back, knowing that the little shit is probably right. A cavern is not the place for an old woman to keel over. (Or maybe it's just the right place.) So, I climb into the wheelchair, which is so narrow that I can barely wedge my fat rump into it.

"I've got you, mumma," says John as he latches on to the handle grips.

"Thank you, John," I say, reaching back to touch his hand. Oh well, since he doesn't mind, I might as well just enjoy the ride.

Before we head into the caverns, we visit the restrooms, and then stop at the snack bar where John hastily devours what I believe to be his first-ever subterranean hot dog. (See? Travel does expand your horizons!) A few minutes later, it is announced that the tour group is heading out.

As we enter, I realize that this will be nothing like my other cave experience. John and I and the kids once visited Carlsbad Caverns in New Mexico, where we waited hours for sunset at the mouth of the cave, when the bats would come out to gorge themselves on insects. (Only when you stop thinking about sunset, stop remembering to look, does it occur.) When the bats finally emerged, there were thousands and thousands of them, darkening, devouring the puce-purple sky. It was a terrifying and beautiful sight. Kevin kept his head beneath a beach towel the entire time.

As I said, nothing like that's going to happen here. What gives it away is the first cave, where the floor is actually covered with linoleum, like someone's rumpus room. There are tables and chairs and a sparkly disco ball hanging from the ceiling. I cackle as John pushes me along.

"Some cave," I say, loud enough for the other six or seven people on the tour to hear. They all look over at us. Yes, I'm being a pill, but I don't care.

Our guide, a chubby young woman with stringy beige hair, deep circles under her eyes, and a bad cold, ignores me and begins her spiel in a nasal, singsongy voice. "In this cave here, which we call 'the ballroom,' we used to have dances back in the 1940s and '50s. Can you imagine young men and women jitterbugging in a cave? Today, it is still available for rental."

Wonderful. A commercial.

As we move deeper into the caverns, the linoleum eventually gives way to a lightly cobbled path that makes my wheelchair vibrate. There are long periods where our guide doesn't say a word, she just croups in a loud, honking way that echoes around us. The caves get darker, and she casually flips light switches as she walks. We roll past long rooms of quivering underground pools, giant oozing stone formations, murky deep grottoes, all with lurid colors projected upon them—infectious reds, virulent ambers, bilious greens. These nasty shades disturb me, especially projected on the stalactites, suspended like daggers from the cavern ceilings, bleeding limestone. I close my eyes, but it only makes me imagine my insides, as they are now, ugly and encrusted with matter. When I open them moments later, I immediately see an enormous shadow of two figures up on the wall of a cave. At first I think we're the shadow, but then I see illuminated statues of Frank and Jesse James in their secret hideout below.

"Be careful, John," I say, pointing out some wet patches on the path.

He says nothing, just pushes me along, nice as you please. Our guide leads us to a medium-sized cave with a lit stone bed. The sign on it says:

TV'S "PEOPLE ARE FUNNY"
HONEYMOON ROOM

Our guide croups and gives us a big fake smile. "Art Linkletter, funnyman that he was, once made a newlywed couple sleep in this cave for nine nights so they could win a vacation in the Bahamas on his television show."

"Are you kidding?" I say out loud. The people around me nod.

"No, it's true. They stayed nine whole nights so they could win a beautiful honeymoon vacation."

"That would be horrible," says a tiny woman in her sixties, to my left.

"That's not funny, that's just plain old mean," I say.

Everyone in the group murmurs in agreement. The crowd is on my side now. I hear someone say, *"That son of a bitch."*

The guide flashes an even broader fake smile and leads us away, before an anti–Art Linkletter revolt breaks out. As we roll forward, she keeps talking. Now we can't shut her up.

"Lester Dill, the man who promoted the caverns for many years, was actually very kind to young couples. In fact, in 1961, he once offered a free wedding to any couples that would agree to get married in the caves. It was a huge success. Thirty-two couples signed up."

She looks over at me, expecting me to spout off, but I'm bored with rabble-rousing and I just smile at her. Why anyone would want to get married in a cave is beyond me. When John and I got hitched, we just did it like everybody did back then. A simple ceremony at the church in my neighborhood, a little party at my aunt Carrie's house, our parents, our friends, a cake my mother made, some sandwiches and coffee. Just a small celebration, not the kind of show-offy affairs they make of weddings these days with cathedrals and halls and limousines. Cindy's wedding almost sent us to the poorhouse, and it didn't even take. What's the point of all that madness, I ask you? All the fancy weddings in the world don't prepare you for where you end up—getting rolled around in a wheelchair through a garish tourist cave by the man who is the father of your children. But before you know it, there you are.

Surprise! There's another depressing little hellhole on Route 66—Cuba, Missouri. In my guidebooks, I read about the past glories of these sad hamlets. In Cuba, there was a place called

"The Midway," a giant complex with a hotel, a car dealership, and a twenty-four-hour restaurant that fed up to six hundred people a day. Now, there's a one-person fruit stand. Go figure.

"John, stop at this stand. I want to buy some grapes."

John pulls the van up to a small clapboard stand where they are selling fresh grapes and grape juice. Apparently, this is wine country and we are here during the harvest.

"Why don't you just stay in the car, John?"

"All right, Ella. Is there anything to drink there?"

"I'll get us some grape juice, okay?"

John nods at me. "Sounds good."

"Don't take off without me," I say as a little joke, but I kind of really mean it. Either way, John is mostly resistant to humor now. He can still make me laugh, whether he knows it or not, but my jokes, such as they are, miss him completely.

I pick out a small bag of grapes and a quart of grape juice, dark as blood. The woman at the stand puts them both in a paper bag for me. "Here you go, darlin'," she says, with the kind of sugar smile that I'm sure is only reserved for adorable old women like myself, eccentrics who wear baseball caps as they waddle charmingly over with their canes from their heavily decaled recreational vehicles. (John always had a weakness for those stickers with the state name in bold letters and "Land of Wonder" or some such motto beneath it. The rear end of the Leisure Seeker is barnacled with them.)

Not that I doubt her sincerity. I don't. I'm always pleased to see a kind face these days, and especially attached to someone bearing food.

"Thank you, miss," I say, as I hand over the dollar bills, unable to conjure up the same regional graciousness.

"You have a good day, ma'am."

There is a burr in her voice, a midwestern flatness that I did not expect here in the middle of the Ozarks, but find quite comforting. We midwesterners, I think, sometimes notice other folks' accents more readily, because ours is, in many ways, so nondescript. But when I hear the variants of our hard *r*'s and nasally twang, it makes me appreciate our native tongue, the planklike dialect that matches our terrain.

We sit for a while in the van and sip juice, eat grapes, along with some Chicken in a Biskit crackers. It's an odd combination, one that I'm not sure I approve of, but I didn't feel like rooting around in the back for anything more substantial. Anyway, I'm just happy to have an appetite. The grapes are luscious, dark and juicy, so I tuck a napkin under my collar as I eat. Neither of us says anything. John occasionally makes a small approving grunt, but that's it. It's good this way, good that we're not speaking. Speaking would only ruin it. For a moment, I am so happy I could cry. This is exactly the sort of thing that makes traveling wonderful for me, the reason I defied everyone. The two of us together like we have always been, not saying anything, not doing anything special, just *on vacation*. I know nothing lasts, but even when you know that things are just about over, sometimes you can run back and take a little bit more and no one will notice.

═══

We drive an old, old stretch of 66—curbed, pinkish, and veined with tar—until it turns into Teardrop Road, which takes us to the Devil's Elbow, a twisty route over a rusted iron suspension bridge across the Big Piney River. Names like "Big Piney River" make me smile, remind me that I am nowhere near my birthplace, where the rivers have names like Rouge and St. Clair. (It occurs to me how French and fancy these names sound. Let me assure you that Detroit is neither. Even in the '50s, when it was booming, it was a tough industrial town, fat with swagger and edged with grime. Yet I can't imagine my life occurring anywhere else but where it did.)

After a bathroom and gas stop in Arlington, Route 66 disappears and we are forced back on I-44. Though the books tell us how to get back onto the old road after a short distance, we cheat a little and stay on the interstate. At yet another Springfield, I direct us back onto the old road.

"How are you feeling, John? You doing all right?"

John nods, runs a hand over his head, then wipes his hand on his sleeve. "I'm all right."

"You tired? Want to find a place to stop for the night?" I'm asking him, but I suspect it's me that really wants to call it a day. I feel sore and shaky. I am experiencing *discomfort*.

"Yeah, okay."

Of course, once we decide to stop, we can't find a place to stay to save our lives. We meander through a braid of towns with curious names: Plew, Rescue, and Albatross; old places of log and stone. In a town called Carthage, we find a campground that will do. We pay our money and set up shop for the night.

The late afternoon sun is too intense, so we sit at our table inside the Leisure Seeker. I turn on a little fan, take my afternoon meds, and settle in to read an old *Detroit Free Press*. After a while, John goes to the back of the van to lie down. The van shifts slightly with his movement. Something creaks in the undercarriage.

"Ella, where are the kids?"

"They're at home."

John sits up in bed, stares wide-eyed at the seam where the paneling meets the ceiling. "We left them there?"

"Uh-huh." I know what's coming.

He twists his head now, searching for me, eyes frantic with fear. "For Christ's sake, we left the kids alone?"

I slap down the paper, in no mood for this. "John, the kids are adults. They've got families of their own now. They have their own houses. They're fine."

"They are?" he says, not quite believing.

"Yes. Don't you remember? Kevin and Cindy both got married. Kevin and Arlene have got two boys, Peter and Steven. And Cindy has a boy and a girl."

"They do?"

"Yes, John. Don't you remember? Their names are Lydia and Joey."

"Oh yeah. They're little kids."

"Joey's eighteen. Lydia's in college. Remember going to her high school graduation?"

Sometimes it feels like all I ever say is "Don't you remember?" to John. I know that somewhere inside of his head, floating around, are all these memories of our life together. I refuse to believe that they are gone. They just need to be coaxed out. And if they need to be nagged out, then so be it.

"Lydia gave a little speech at graduation, about knowing where you're heading, finding your own way into the future? Everyone applauded? Joey played in the band at the ceremony?"

"Yeah, I remember."

"Well, good. You should remember. Keep remembering it because I'm goddamn sick and tired of remembering everything for you."

"I'm sorry, Ella," he says, shamed.

Sometimes I just want to smack myself. "Oh, shit. I'm sorry, too, honey. I didn't mean to get mad."

"It's this memory of mine."

"I know, dear."

I turn the page and decide to tackle the Jumble. I look around for a pencil.

"Ella, where are the kids?"

Deep breath. "They're fine, John. Why don't you take a nap?"

So, I tell him to take a nap and what happens? I fall asleep at the table. Involuntary catnaps: it's another reason why getting old is for the birds. You don't mean to fall asleep, but then suddenly you wake up and hours have passed. It's an entirely different time of day. There's a gap, an in-between period you just can't account for.

It's pitch-black in the van now and it scares me. John and I have not let it get completely dark in our house for years. These days, it disorients him and it just plain spooks me. When we go to bed, we always leave lights on all over the house. We sleep in half-dark rooms, doze in shadows. We live there, in the half night, especially John.

"John!" I yell, trying not to panic. He's snoring to beat the band. Finally, I remember that there's a lamp right over the table. Jesus. I reach up and fumble around till I find the switch. The light makes me safe again.

"John, get up." I look at my watch.

"What is it?" he says, voice sticky with sleep.

"We've been snoozing for almost three hours. It's dark outside." I try to get up, but my legs are asleep. I wiggle my feet to get the circulation started. "Could you help me?"

"Just a second," he says. In a moment, he's at the table, his hands outstretched to pull me.

"Ow, ow, ow." The edge of the table scrapes my belly. "Old Two-Ton Tessie here." Then I'm back on my feet, knees discomforting like crazy.

"Hush," John says, smoothing back my hair. His hands smell vinegary, but I welcome his touch.

"I'm okay. You hungry?"

John brightens at the mention of food. He's in good post-nap spirits. Sometimes he wakes up mean as the devil. It can go either way.

"Why don't I make us some eggs and bacon?" I say.

"Good deal."

I shuffle to the kitchenette, all of three steps. (This is why RVs are the cat's ass. When you get old, everything gets farther away. But here in the Leisure Seeker, everything's right there where you need it.)

I fire up the electric frying pan, pull bacon and eggs out of the icebox, and lay six strips in the pan. After I hound him into washing his hands, John is on toast detail. He stands at the counter, a stack of Wonder bread in front of him.

"Don't put it in the toaster yet," I say.

I watch as he closes up the bag with a twist tie and starts rummaging in our junk drawer till he finds the scissors. He then snips the excess plastic bag just above the twist tie. John has done this for the last couple years. It's the sickness. At home, he was always stacking, straightening, fiddling with something. He'd trim the bag, leave the room, then come back in and do it again. Sometimes before we even use any of the bread, the bag is trimmed down to a nub. Despite this, he's more lucid than usual and all this feels pretty normal.

"Hey, how about a cocktail?" I say.

"Sounds good."

I know you're probably thinking, she's grateful for a precious few moments of clearheadedness with her husband and what does she do? Make him dull with booze. You would have a point, but I really don't care. I reach up into a cupboard and pull out bottles of Canadian Club and sweet vermouth.

"We haven't had a cocktail hour in a long time," I say as I turn the bacon on low. "Get some ice out of the cooler."

John surprises me by turning on the tape player to some music. The van is suddenly filled with the sounds of lush strings and a mellow baritone sax. Years ago, he taped a lot of our favorite albums for us to listen to on vacations. All kinds of good stuff—Arthur Lyman, Tony Mottola, Herb Alpert, Jackie Gleason.

"Is that 'Midnight Sun'?" I ask.

"I guess," he says, coming back with a tray of ice cubes.

"I think it is." I mix us manhattans, extra sweet. After the kids left home, John and I started having a little drink before dinner. We would sit downstairs at our rumpus room bar where we used to entertain, light a candle, put on some music, and just chat. John was just finishing up as an engineer at GM then and he would tell me about what was going on over at the Tech Center, who was stabbing who in the back, who was getting laid off, and so on. He didn't care anymore since he was retiring. (Thank God for "Thirty and Out." It was the mid-'80s, just as the Detroit auto industry was going to hell in a handbasket.) I would tell him who I had talked to that day, what was going on in the kids' lives, sales at the grocery store—nothing earthshaking. But we got things out there, shared information.

Now we sit around our table staring at our drinks without a word. I'm thankful for Andy Williams singing "Moon River." At least someone's saying something. I give my drink a swirl, watch the cherry drop to the bottom. I lift my glass. "Well, here's mud in your eye."

John raises his glass and smiles, like he always has. Is there such a thing as cocktail muscle memory? I take a sip. It's cold, sweet, and strong, and I remember that there is nothing like that first sip of a cocktail. Ah! The pleasure of forgetting, then finding again. This gives me renewed hope for the idea of this trip. John sips his drink and squeezes his eyes shut. I worry for a moment, then he sighs contentedly. "God damn, that's good."

"We're making progress, don't you think?"

John nods. "Sure are."

"I think we did maybe about three hundred miles today."

John takes a second sip and frowns. "Doesn't seem like very much."

"We're doing fine. It's just slower taking the old road. Don't you worry."

"Maybe tomorrow," he says.

"Maybe tomorrow," I repeat, raising my glass. And never have two words seemed so true.

After our dinner, I decide that we need something else to do. I give John a Pepsi and make myself another drink. "Time for the evening's entertainment."

"It is?" says John, rolling a toothpick in his mouth.

John didn't know that I packed the projector and a big box of slides. At home, in our basement, there's a cabinet stacked with trays of slides—vacations, family reunions, weekend outings, birthday parties, weddings, new babies, everything that's ever happened to us. At one time, John was quite the shutter-bug. He was our official family photographer.

It's a balmy night, and I like the idea of watching slides outdoors like at a drive-in. A floodlight has just ticked on nearby, so it's not so dangerously dark. I leave the lights on in the van, which spreads a warm glow over our campsite yet is still dim enough to use the projector that I have John lug to the picnic table.

"How you doing out there, John?" I yell out to him.

"Where's the screen?"

"Uh-oh. I forgot to bring one. I'll get a sheet."

I rummage around in our little cardboard storage chest and find a bunch of them, orphans left over from sets that wore out long ago. I'm not prepared for how they make me feel. Seeing these old sheets right now, rubbed so smooth, washed hundreds of times over the years, I can't help but think of my life, or at least my married life, in terms of linens: the spotted stiff white wedding gift linens of our first hungry years together; those same sheets yellow with urine from Cindy climbing into bed with us; the pastel sheets I picked out after eighteen or nineteen years of marriage (that time where early components of a union need replacing—mattresses, radios, towels, all falling apart at the same time—reminding you of just how long it's been); those same replacement sheets following us into middle age; then newer striped cotton-blend linens from the outlet malls we would encounter on the road (the luxury of three or four sets to choose from), taking us into deep middle age, then agedness, these last linens now softened to silk by constant scrubbing, lately soiled by John's gradual lack of hygiene, the smell of an unwashed body preparing itself for a long slumber.

I think of my closet full of linens at home being sold at an estate sale. When I used to go to the sales, I never even considered buying anyone's linens. Old sheets are just too personal, too full of dreams.

I pull out an old white sheet, almost worn through, that will suit our purposes nicely. I step outside to find John at the picnic table, quietly weeping.

"John, what's wrong?"

He looks up at me, eyes red and wet, brimming with frustration. "Ella, Goddamn it. I can't get this thing started."

It disturbs me to see him cry. "Sweetie, it's all right. Let me see." I look around and find that he has plugged the extension cord to the outside outlet, but has not connected the projector cord to the extension cord. "It's okay. You just forgot to plug this in."

John lifts his glasses, uses the heels of his hands to wipe his eyes, pressing hard into the sockets. "*Goddamn* this memory of mine."

I kiss my husband's cheek and hand him a Kleenex from my sleeve. "Come on. Let's watch some slides."

It's a long sunset over Lake St. Clair. Our daughter, Cindy, is lounging on a dock in her middle teens. We can see only her silhouette, her then-new young woman's body set against the sky, which is fiery orange and gold with streaks of periwinkle. The colors seem artificial now, sharpened red with time, hyper-real like the colors of my dreams, on those occasions when they are in color. (As old as I feel, I'm sometimes surprised that my dreams are talkies.) It was a cottage where we spent many summer weekends, one that we shared with my brother and sisters and their families.

"Who's that, John?" I ask, testing him. "Do you know who that is?"

"Of course I do. It's Cynthia."

"That's right." I'm holding the remote button. I click to the next slide. There is a shot of the four of us all together, a lovely one that John must have taken with the self-timer on the camera. We are all gathered in our shorts and bright-colored shirts and blouses after a long day outdoors. We look sunburned and happy, except for Cindy, who is sulking, most likely over some boy.

"That's a nice shot, John."

"Yeah."

A few slides later, we are in the kitchen of the old cottage. My baby brother Ted and his wife, Stella, are there with their three kids, Terry, Ted Jr., and Tina. (Some parents are determined to alphabetize their offspring and there is no way to talk them out of it. I always felt bad for Stella, being one letter off from the pack.) My older sister Lena is there as well with her brood. Al, her soak of a husband, was probably off getting sloshed in the garage. He spent most of his time there, near the beer fridge. (Cirrhosis, when it happened, was no surprise to any of us.)

"Looks like a party," John says.

"Just dinnertime."

In the slide, people are standing around a table, helping themselves. The table is covered with lunch meats and potato chips and macaroni salads, Jell-O salads, bowls of dips and crackers, bottles of pop (red, orange, green) with names that I barely recognize: Uptown and Wink and Towne Club. I think about dozens of other photos like this one over the years, huge spreads of food, tables covered with it. I think about the people in the slides, most of them gone now, heart attacks and cancers, betrayed by the foods we ate, by our La-Z-Boys, by our postwar contentment, everyone getting larger and larger in every year's photographs, our prosperity gone wide.

Tonight, though, what makes this particular photo interesting to me is *me*. (Why are we always attracted to the image of ourselves in a photograph? This doesn't change, even at my age.) I'm in the background of the photo, standing in a corner, staring off to the side, not talking to anyone.

"You were sad that night," says John, out of nowhere.

I'm surprised that he would say this. But looking at the slide again, I realize that I do look sad. "I was? What was I sad about?"

"I don't know."

Suddenly, I want to know the cause of my sadness. It becomes very important to me to know, but I can't remember.

Behind us, on the road, a young family stops and waves. The husband, a dark-haired athletic fellow in his thirties, smiles robustly like he knows us.

"How you doing there?" he says, tugging his reluctant little towhead boy our way. His wife, a pert blonde in a pink sundress, follows behind, indulging her chatty husband in a way that looks mighty familiar to me.

The wife kneels down to the boy, points up at the screen. "See, honey, that's what things looked like in the olden days."

The boy, who looks about seven, is wearing a T-shirt that says: BEEN THERE, DONE THAT, BOUGHT THE T-SHIRT.

I recognize the look on his face. He wants to escape, probably to go play with his Game Boy, if he's anything like my grandkids.

"Nice setup you've got here," says the husband.

"We like it," I say. Somehow, I can't bring myself to say much more. I'm hoping John will say something, but he's concentrating on the screen. A few years back, you wouldn't have been able to shut him up. John used to love to gab with strangers. He and this fellow would have gotten on famously, chewing the fat about the weather or camping or our respective destinations. But now, John sits in silence. The family stays for a few slides, then says good-bye. I'm glad when they leave, slightly annoyed with the blonde's comment about "the olden days," but mostly just ashamed of myself for my envy of their youth, of their lives so full and unfolding before them, of their complete unawareness of their great good fortune.

Some other folks walk by, and I have to say they get bored pretty quickly with our lives projected up there. Then a man and a woman in their late sixties come by. They stand and watch for quite some time. I can tell it's not just a quaint amusement to them. This is probably what their life looks like, too.

When our kids were growing up, their idea of hell was to watch slides. When Cindy was a teenager, she couldn't run from the living room fast enough when we'd drag out the projector. Kevin wasn't much better. I'd make them watch for ten or fifteen minutes, then they'd get so fidgety that I'd let them go off so John and I could watch in peace. But in the past few years, both kids have come around. They like watching slides now and so do their children. I think they've realized that this is their history. It's the history of all of us.

Up on the screen it is a different day on that same summer weekend, a barbecue with everyone outside playing catch, children doing somersaults for the camera, everyone loading up on hot dogs, hamburgers, mustard potato salad, three-bean salad, and ambrosia salad. The other cottages behind the people in the slides look bland and generic, like theatrical backdrops meant only to fill the eye. During a horseshoe match, I am far in the background again, looking no cheerier than before, yet John kept including me in his shots. I don't know why. Then I remember something. I remember John waving at me from behind the camera that day, trying to cheer me up. It was shortly after my third miscarriage, the baby I had carried for so long, then so suddenly lost. Crushed, I had given up on having a second child at that point. A weekend party was the last place I wanted to be, but John and my sister Lena thought it would be good for me.

Even though I know the ending to this story and it's a happy one—I changed doctors, and a year and a half later I gave birth to Kevin—it still wounds me to see that pained young woman up there trapped in her horrible present. I stop clicking forward and continue to stare at my blurry, background self. I am barely recognizable as I start to dissolve. I don't proceed to the next slide. The oldsters wave good-bye to us and head back down the road, probably thinking that I'm nuts. They may be right. We've barely watched a tray and a half of slides, but I think we're done for the night.

Five

KANSAS

After passing the Route 66 Flea Market, the Route 66 Drive-in, the Route 66 Salvage Yard, another Route 66 Diner, and the Route 66 Bookstore, we enter Kansas. I'll say this: there may only be twelve miles of Route 66 in Kansas, but they are very well marked. Not only are there "Historic 66" signs everywhere, but the 66 insignia is also painted on the road practically every ten feet. They don't miss a trick.

Yet the joy of crossing a state line is short-lived. John and I soon find ourselves in "Hell's Half Acre," a dire, barren landscape of coarse scrub, welts of dried muck, and random piles of crushed rock. My guidebook says this stretch of land was permanently damaged and depleted by years and years of strip mining. I don't like this place one bit. It makes me think of smiling, cruel-faced men cutting into the earth, ripping everything out, all the while telling you something good will come of it, but leaving only scar tissue.

I feel for that earth. After a lifetime's worth of appendectomies, episiotomies, cesareans, hysterectomies, lumpectomies, hip replacements, knee replacements, endarterectomies, and catheterizations, the landscape of my body is its own Hell's Half Acre. (More like a whole acre in my case.) A topographical map of stitches, scars, staple marks, and the sundry etchings of medical procedure. So this time, when the doctors were, for once, loath to slash me open, you can see why I was glad. You can see why I had to take off with my husband and hit the road. Sooner or later, enough is enough.

Here's how it works: doctors like to save people, but when you're talking about someone who's eighty years old, what the hell is there left to save? What fun is it to cut *them* open? They'll do it if you really want, yet they're sure to let you know of the complications. The dastardly buggers pull out tongue twisters like "comorbidities." It's a word that takes you a while to figure out, but once you do, it makes perfect sense. It's the horse race between the things that are eventually going to do you in: *Coming up to the stretch, in the lead is Metastasized Breast Cancer! Second is Advanced Hypertension, behind him, Carotid Blockage is a distant third with Kidney Failure bringing up the rear. Oh! But coming on strong is Ischemic Stroke! Now Stroke is neck and neck with Breast Cancer! Stroke, Cancer! Cancer, Stroke! Ladies and Gentlemen, what a race!*

Besides Eisler Brothers' Grocery Store, the only pleasant sight my guidebooks and maps mention is an old bridge referred to as a "Marsh Rainbow Arch." There used to be three of these long, elegant rainbow-shaped 1920s bridges in Kansas, but the other two were torn down, so now there's only the one left. I direct John toward it. In no time at all, we see a lovely little concrete bridge, a long arching span, recently painted white, over a short drink of a creek. Someone has stenciled the 66 insignia at the end of the rainbow. There's no one around for miles, so in the middle of it, I tell John to stop the van.

"What?" says John, not sure if he's hearing me right.

"Stop the truck, John."

Once he does, I open my door and get out. I go stand out on this tiny bridge that links the two sides of Brush Creek.

"For Pete's sake, what are you doing?" says John, peeved.

I don't know, but all I want to do right now is stand here for a moment. According to the photos I've seen, the other two bridges were much bigger and even lovelier. They were destroyed simply because someone thought they needed something new and bland. Why does the world have to destroy anything that doesn't fit in? We still can't figure out that this is the most important reason to love something.

I feel at home here braced between shores. It's how I feel these days, stuck between here and there, dark and light, heaviness and weightlessness. I lean over the edge of the bridge and try to peer deep into the water, but it's dark and murky.

"Ella!"

"Just a *second*." I look down the creek and spot something along the side. It's a creature of some sort—cat or muskrat or beaver, with a kind of slick black fur. Whatever it is, it's been dead for a long time. I don't know if this is what made me want to stop and look, but if it is, I'm sorry I did. A vision of death is not what I needed. In fact, seeing it makes me fumble myself back in the van, holding on to every extra handle John has jerry-rigged over the years, faster than I can usually move these days.

"Let's get the hell out of here, John."

We pass through Baxter Springs. Shortly afterward, there is a sign that says WELCOME TO OKLAHOMA.

"That was fast," John says.

This is how quickly we go through Kansas. Even John notices.

"I'll say. We're really making great time today," I say, smiling at him. He smiles back. He seems good this morning, so it's a surprise when he says what he says to me.

"Ella, have you seen my gun around?"

Six

OKLAHOMA

I'm not really sure what to say. His gun is here in the Leisure Seeker, but I know he doesn't know where it is. I made sure of that. Anyway, it's really *our* gun and we've always traveled with one, especially the last twenty years. It's quite illegal taking a firearm across state lines, but we need something to protect ourselves.

I suppose that I should explain right here that sometimes John, in his more lucid moments, wants to kill himself. He has not said this to me in so many words, mind you, but I know that is what he is thinking.

Decades back, John's mother had the same disease he has now, only then they called it "hardening of the arteries." He was not terribly close to his mother, but her illness made a huge impression on him. Truth be told, she was an unpleasant woman who believed that the world owed her much more than she ever received. I don't believe that she was ever really close to anyone, not her two husbands, not her son or daughter, and she certainly wasn't close to me. Even still, it hurt John terribly to watch her turn into something that was much worse than his unhappy mother. Toward the end of her time at home, she would be up and down all night, wandering her neighborhood, prone to fits of rage and apoplexy.

We started getting late-night calls from her second husband, Leonard, a gentle, easily defeated man, pleading for our help. After she ended up in the nursing home (and this was the early days of nursing homes, where they had the genuine look of hell to them), John said he would never end up in one of those places, made me swear that I would never put him in one, no matter what happened to him. He told me that he would kill himself first, if he ever thought he was going senile.

It was about a year ago when I started finding the gun stashed in strange places in our house—sock drawer, kitchen cupboard, magazine rack—I was terrified. I'd ask him about it, but he never knew how it got there. The problems were getting worse then, and I knew that people in his condition tend to think everyone's after them, so I hid the gun for good. He kept asking me if I'd seen it, sometimes three or four times a day. Then he just seemed to forget about it. I was relieved until a few months later when I found a half-written suicide note stuffed between the pages of one of his favorite Louis L'Amour books, *The Proving Trail*. I couldn't decipher a lot of it, but I got the gist. As you can imagine, it was pretty upsetting. But how upset should you get over a suicide note where the person seems to lose interest in the middle?

As I've said before, these days, John only occasionally realizes that he is losing his mind. I think that's when he asks about his gun. This is the evil, damnable, and lucky thing about his sickness. By the time he finds the gun, he has forgotten what he wanted it for.

"I've seen it, John, but I just can't remember where it is."

"Is it in the van?"

"I don't know, John. I just can't remember things like I used to. You know how that is." I glance at him, and he seems satisfied at this explanation.

"Look at that, John," I say, pointing to the side of the road at the telephone poles, splintered and crooked, that have been following the road for some time. This line of drunken soldiers has suddenly veered off to the right out of sight.

"Where do you suppose they're headed to?"

John says nothing. I know he's still thinking about that gun while he can, before his mind hits the reset button. Stiffly, I chatter on, trying to fill the air, fill his head, with words. "I read about those poles in my guidebooks," I say. "The telephone lines are following an old alignment of Route 66, but there's no road there now. There are a lot of different old stretches of the highway. They kept changing it over the years. Sometimes the road goes though towns that don't even exist anymore."

John nods, but not at me blathering on about forgotten

roads leading to phantom towns. He is having one of his arguments with himself, telling off whomever it was that stole his gun. He's following his own forgotten road.

I'm wishing the wandering line of phone poles would return because I want to follow them, find out where they would take us. A ghost town sounds good to me, a fine place to set up shop. I roll down my window a little farther, pull off my cap, and drag a brush through my hair. The bristles scratch my scalp, but it feels good. I pull the greasy strays, the opaque flecks of skin from the brush and release them into the wind. I rummage through the glove box until I find a rubber band, which I use to make a short pigtail. This is how I will wear my hair now, I decide, thinning or not. I put the hat behind the seat. I'm tired of looking eccentric. I have not lived an eccentric life.

"Mother, where are you?"

I'm talking to my frantic son this morning. I had John stop for a moment in Miami, Oklahoma, to take a quick look at a beautiful old theater there, the Coleman. (It put me in mind of the Vanity Ballroom off Jefferson Avenue in Detroit, where I used to go dancing during the war. Me and three girlfriends along with dozens of other girls and their girlfriends, and a few 4-F fellas pleased with the odds.) When we drove past, I spied a phone booth and decided to call.

"We're in Oklahoma, Kevin."

"Everyone is so worried about you two. I'm going to fly out there and pick you up."

I have steeled myself for this battle. "No, you're not. Your father and I are having a wonderful time, but we don't wish you were here."

Kevin takes a long breath and exhales loudly through his mouth. I can feel his shoulders slump, right over the phone. "Mom, we are very close to calling the police and filing a Missing Persons report."

"Don't you *dare,* Kevin!" I mean it, too.

He sighs. "Mom. This is crazy. Why are you doing this?"

"Dear. Because we want to. It's so nice to be traveling again, I can't tell you."

"Really?" he says, his tone changing, allowing a hint of enthusiasm. But a moment later, his voice grows frantic again. "Wait, wasn't there some kind of problem with the van? Something with the exhaust manifold?"

"Oh, we got that fixed ages ago, honey."

"Are you sure?" he says, not quite believing me. "That could be dangerous."

"Don't worry, Kevin. Everything's working just the way it should be."

He sighs again, even louder this time. I don't mean for this to be hard on him, but Kevin is forever upset about something. Even when he was a child, he was always sad or guilty or crying about something. Cindy took care of herself. Kevin was the sensitive one. You learn these things about your children: their personalities reveal themselves the moment out of the womb.

I suppose he was a mama's boy, but I can't say I cared. I wished he didn't cry so much, but I was glad when he came to me for comfort. Yet John would get so upset with him. He was afraid the world would eat him alive, and he was right. Bullies could spot Kevin six blocks away. He was always coming home with something broken, something stolen, something thrown in the mud. John tried to toughen him up—pep talks, boxing lessons—but it never seemed to take. He kept trying to get Kevin to not be afraid, to put up his dukes, but it was no use. Those dukes were down.

Even now, Kevin tells me stories about the company where he works, a place that distributes replacement engine parts for one of the Big Three, how his coworkers take advantage of him, bully him. Some things never change.

"You gotta come home, Mom. Are you taking your medications?"

"Of course I am." This is mostly the truth.

"Oh Mom." Another sigh.

So now, I've had it. "Damn it, Kevin. Stop being such a sad sack. We're not coming home. What do you want me to come home to? More doctor appointments? More treatments? More drugs? I take so many right now, they're going to turn me into a dope addict. No. There will be no coming home. Do you understand?"

One final sigh. "Yes. I understand."

"Good. Now, how's Arlene and the boys?"

A pause. "They're good. How's Dad? Is he okay?"

"He's fine, honey. He's driving great and he's doing really well. Don't worry so much about us. We need to do this."

"Okay. Just be careful."

I see John futzing around with something in the van across the street and think I need to get over there pretty quick.

"Bye-bye. Give our love to everyone."

"Mom—"

I hang up in time to watch John start to put the van in gear. For the love of Christ, I think he's going to drive away without me. The Leisure Seeker lurches forward a few feet, and I scream John's name as loudly as I can. People on the street stop and look at me. I want to run, but I can't run. My knees won't do it. I wave my cane at the van.

"Someone please stop that truck!" I screech.

A young man wearing mechanic's overalls comes up to me. The patch over his right pocket reads MAL. His hands are filthy, but he's got a kind smile and he speaks gently to me. "Do you need help, ma'am?"

"Yes. Could you run up to that van and tell the man to wait for me?"

Without even looking both ways, the young man runs off into the street toward the van, which is moving slowly down the street. But before he gets around to the driver's side, the van stops. He disappears around the side, so I can't see what's going on, but I hightail it across the street, as much as I can hightail it.

Once I get to the passenger door, the young man is talking

to John through the window. "It's fine, ma'am," he says. "He wasn't going anywhere. May I give you a hand?" He opens the door for me.

"Thank you so much, Mal. You're a doll."

Mal smiles at me, offers me a filthy hand, and I gladly accept it. I notice the patch over his left pocket as he helps me up. It's a Phillips 66 insignia. I guess The Road provides. I step up into the van, close the door, and wave. I wait until we're a good ways down the street before I speak.

"What are you, *nuts*?" I scream at John. "You going to take off without me? Where are you going to go? What are you gonna do? You'd be lost without me, you goddamned idiot." I feel my blood pressure rising. "Where were you going to go? Huh? Tell me. What? You stupid asshole."

John looks at me, a mixture of anger and befuddlement. "I wasn't going anywhere. I just thought I heard a noise, so I drove forward for a couple of feet. For Christ's sake, I wouldn't take off without you."

"Well, you goddamn well better not. Crazy old man."

"Up yours," says John.

I grab a Kleenex from our dispenser and wipe my hand. "Up your own."

No one says anything for the next dozen or so miles. After that, John turns to me and smiles. "Hi, honey," he says, putting his hand on my knee.

This little greeting is something we've always done, shorthand for "I'm glad you're here," "You're dear to me," or something to that effect. Whatever it means, I am not in the mood for it right now. I move my knee out of reach.

"Go to hell."

"Why?"

"I'm still mad at you." I cross my arms. "You almost took off without me."

"What?"

God, how I hate it when he does this. We get into an argument and start screaming at each other, then five minutes later, he's forgotten all about it. He's all lovey-dovey. What do you do when someone forgets to stay mad? How do you fight with that? You don't. You just shut up because it'll make you crazy.

"You were gonna take off without me, dumbass." I guess knowing what you need to do is different from actually doing it.

"You're crazy. Go screw yourself."

That makes me feel better. We're both angry now, the way it should be. There's another silence for about a minute, then John turns to me.

"Hi, honey," he says.

I sigh. "Hi, John."

It was my granddaughter who first noticed the changes in John's behavior. During a Christmas celebration at our house about four years back, she found John downstairs in our rumpus room, where we keep all the memorabilia of our vacations, including a mounted map of the United States where John has marked the routes in color-coded tape. According to Lydia, he was walking around, bewildered, looking at everything and muttering to himself, "It's going to be hard leaving all this."

Lydia walked up to him and said, "Grandpa, are you all right?" She said that he looked at her as if he wasn't sure who exactly she was. When she repeated the question, he just nodded.

Then she asked him, "Where are you going, Grandpa? You said you have to leave all this."

He just said, "Nowhere. I'm not going anywhere."

By the time Lydia got him upstairs, he seemed all right, more like himself, but she took me aside and told me what happened.

When I asked John about it later, he denied it. He was sure that he hadn't even been downstairs, but I had seen him come up myself. Nothing happened for a couple of months after that, so I managed to push it out of my mind.

Then we went to Florida. We were headed to Kissimmee to visit friends who had a condo down there. All along the way, John had indigestion and light-headedness and shortness of breath. He kept saying he was all right, but I didn't believe him. Midway into our second day of driving (we were trying to make it there in two days, always the big rush), he pulled over to the side of the freeway, panting. Then he opened the door and threw up.

"John, what's wrong?" I was really scared by this time.

"I don't know, I don't know!" He was coughing and wheezing by then. "I can't breathe, Ella!"

I thought he was having a heart attack, but he wasn't holding his chest or his arm or anything like that.

John held his hands over his mouth, breath shallow, eyes welling, voice trembling. "I don't know if I can drive, Ella. I feel so light-headed. I'm afraid."

It was the only time I ever heard him say that to me.

Around then, another Leisure Seeker pulled up behind us. A man in his fifties came up to the window and asked if everything was okay. (Leisure Seeker owners stick together that way.)

"I think my husband's having a heart attack," was what I said.

The man looked at John and saw he was truly sick. "Can you drive your van?" he asked me.

"I haven't driven a car in thirty years, much less this thing," I said.

"Okay." He ran to his RV, then ran back to ours. "I'll drive you two to the next town, and my wife will follow us."

We ended up in some podunk hospital in the Florida panhandle. (It's worth saying here that if you can ever avoid being in a hospital in Florida, do so. Instead of "the Sunshine State," the state motto should be "Land of Unnecessary Surgery.") Some greasy quack admitted John, got him into a bed, examined him, and proclaimed him a candidate for open-heart surgery within ten minutes.

"Bullshit," said John, who was feeling better by then. "No way."

After that, they put the pressure on me. "It's for his own good. He could go at any time." They basically scared the bejesus out of me. I told them I had to call my children. Cindy said the same thing as John. Kevin volunteered to come down the next day. I told the hospital that there wasn't going to be any surgery, not for a while at least.

Kevin arrived the next day. By then, John felt fine. He was ready to resume our trip.

"I'm driving the van back to Detroit," said Kevin, with as much conviction as I'd ever heard from him. "You two are flying home."

We both pissed and moaned because neither of us liked flying, but eventually we relented. It was the first time that we felt a real shift in power, how our kids now felt like they were in charge of us instead of the other way around. It's not a good feeling, let me tell you. Watching the Leisure Seeker pull up in our driveway three days later made me feel like a scolded child banished to home. Grounded.

Our doctor at home, after hearing what happened and a thorough examination, told us that John had what is commonly referred to as an anxiety attack. An *anxiety attack*. Can you imagine?

John laughed it off. I personally didn't really think anyone of our generation could suffer from such a condition. Anxiety was for our children and their children, but not for people who had grown up during the Depression, who had fought in the war. Who has time for anxiety when you're trying to fill your belly or keep your head on?

I see now that the doctor was right. I believe this was when John was starting to truly understand what was happening to him. We have always been worriers, both of us. I'm just more likely to worry out loud. John keeps it in, like a man tends to do. I imagine him realizing with a horrible finality that he was indeed going to end up like his mother. Who knows what triggered it? But I imagine him running it through his head over and over as we drove along. That was enough to leave him breathless and heaving by the side of the road. And that, as they say, was the beginning of the bad times.

We eat lunch at a little barbecue joint called "The Pits" in Claremore. Both John and I feel better now, but then barbecue pork sandwiches will do that. John is an unholy mess with orangey-red sauce and grease smeared on his face and fingers. I look much the same way, I imagine.

This is our trip to eat anything we want. You have to remember, after you achieve a certain age, there are always people telling you what to eat and what not to eat. We start off in this life on milk and pablum, and they'd like to finish us off that way as well. (But without the milk because, you know, *the cholesterol*.) I say all this now, but I know, even with the Pepcid we took in the car, there will be gastric hell to pay later for this barbecue sandwich.

"You two look like you're enjoying yourselves," drawls our

waitress, a rangy middle-aged redhead with too short a skirt, who appears from nowhere.

I smile, wipe the sauce off John's face, then my own.

"More tea, dear?" she says to me, her voice thick and low pitched, already refilling my glass.

I have never been *dear*ed and *darlin*ed so much in my whole life as on this trip. If you've experienced that first middle-aged shock when you become "ma'am" or "sir," it's nothing like when you become "dear."

"No, thank you," I say, smiling back. It doesn't really matter because she has already filled the glass. "My back teeth are already floating."

"Heh, heh."

Normally I wouldn't say anything like that, but I don't seem to care lately.

When she leaves the check, I grab my purse from down between my feet (away from pickpockets and sneak thieves and such) to fetch my wallet. I give the money to John and let him go up to pay. Meanwhile, I hunt down the ladies' room. As I sit there on the pot, I look up and see that someone has written something in a delicate script on the stall door.

Love Always,
Charlie

Who the hell would write something like that in the ladies' room toilet? The world just keeps getting stranger. As I wash my hands, I worry that John has taken off on me, but when I exit the restroom, he's waiting for me, nice as you please, polishing off a Hershey bar and talking to Red like it's old home week.

"We're headed back home to Michigan," John says to her.

"I've never been to Michigan. Is it nice?"

"It's wonderful," says John. "We'll be back in a day or two."

I don't bother to correct him. As I approach, he holds out his arm for me to take. It makes me glad to be married.

We pass on the Will Rogers Memorial in Claremore. I never much cared for the man. A big phony, I believe. Anyone who never met a man he didn't like just isn't trying hard enough. I roll down my window all the way and hang my arm out. The wind tries to push my hand back, but I flatten my palm and hold it strong against the flow for a moment, then dip my hand horizontally, then cup it as if I were swimming. I weave my hand up and down, a reverse sidestroke through the air. There is a strange freedom to this gesture, a childishness, I know, but it feels good to be silly. There is so little silliness at this period of one's life, but it's the time when you need it the most. I cup my flowing hand and keep swimming in the wind and to my surprise, water soon appears along the side of the road—a long swimming hole, with a fringe of bulrushes, and a giant blue whale smack in the middle. Bright as the sky, mouth open and smiling, squealing children diving off his concrete back into the water. I sweep my arm forward and am suddenly swimming with the whales.

Sometimes when you least expect it, your life becomes a National Geographic special.

Before Tulsa, I direct John onto the I-44 bypass. We pick 66 back up at Sapulpa. Suddenly, I've got some considerable discomfort. I want to take a little blue pill, but I don't want to do it until we're settled.

"John," I say, trying not to sound too weary. "I'm tired. Maybe we should find somewhere to stay for the night."

"What time is it?"

The clock in the van has been broken for years. My watch says it's only 3:05, but I don't want to get into it with John about not traveling long enough.

"It's after five," I say, lying to my husband. "Let's keep our eyes peeled for a place." I go into my purse for my little blue pills. I try to break one in half, but it won't break. Against my better judgment, I take the whole thing and wash it down with a sip of Faygo Root Beer.

Within ten minutes or so, I feel a little better, but start getting drowsy. Up ahead, there's a billboard for a gas station in a town called Chandler. I remember something from my guidebooks about a good place to stay there. No sooner do we enter town than I see the sign for the Lincoln Motel.

"John, turn in here. I'd like to sleep in a real bed tonight."

John does what he is told, I'm happy to report. We turn in and park by the office. Even feeling as rotten as I do, I have to say that the place is just darling, an old-time motor hotel from the '30s. Luckily, there's a vacancy.

When we drive along the back to park near our cabin, I notice something. "John, look at all these old cars."

"How about that," he says, giving a little whistle.

I point to one bulbous, bullet-nosed, gray-green car in particular. "John, there's a 1950 Studebaker. Remember? We had one like that a few years after we got married. You taught me how to drive in that car."

"I'll be damned," he says. "That was a good car."

"God, did you scream at me that day. I was so mad at you."

John shakes his head. "You were an awful driver."

I want to tell him to cram it, but the fact is, he's right. I was an awful driver. I never really got the hang of it. I was always afraid of going too fast. I hated freeways and left turns and parallel parking. I was constantly getting yelled at, either by John or people in other cars. Still, it's hard to live in Detroit if you don't drive. Yet as soon as the kids were old enough, I let them drive me everywhere. I gave it up for good right after Kevin got his license.

"There's an old Imperial. That's a beauty," says John, checking out a gaudy lavender boat with gargantuan fins and ringed taillights like gun sights.

Yes, we are definitely from a car town. We park next to a shiny red Ford Pinto with a license plate that says:

IBLOWUP

Our cabin is small, but clean and comfortable and all I want to do is go to bed, but I have to make sure that John is settled in as well.

"Let's take a little nap, John. Then we'll bring in our things."

"I'm not tired."

"Well, I am." I turn on the television to distract him. We start watching an old rerun of *M*A*S*H* and John is immediately absorbed. I swear, he's seen every episode a hundred times, but he still loves to watch them. I think that's why he can still enjoy them. They're familiar, but new. I lock the door, then settle into the too-soft bed, deeply weary.

When I wake up, John is gone. It's only 5:25 P.M., so I haven't been sleeping long. I pray that he has not wandered off somewhere. I swing my legs over the side of the bed and raise myself, using both my cane and the night table. Standing somehow makes me feel better, as if I am fooling my body into vigor. I open the door of our cabin and am relieved to see John sitting on a lawn chair, just staring into space. On a little table next to him is our slide projector.

"John?"

"I set up the projector."

"Good for you, but it's too light to show slides."

"I can see that, Ella." He can still remember to be sarcastic when need be.

"Well, good. We'll set up the sheet in a little while. Come

on, let's go rustle up some sandwiches. I've got ham and bologna. What sounds good?"

"Bologna."

Why do I even ask? He had a bologna sandwich every day for thirty-five years when he was working. Bologna with one slice of American cheese and a smear of mustard, cut top to bottom, not diagonally. I could make them in my sleep.

We walk around back to the van. I hope the projector will be all right because I don't feel like moving it. I make us sandwiches and potato chips and root beer. My discomfort has subsided and I decide to whip myself up an old-fashioned. I dig out the booze, find a couple of desiccated sugar cubes in the cupboard, and I'm in business. I top the whole kit and kaboodle with a skewered orange slice and a cherry. It's not an old-fashioned without. John just gets another glass of pop. The sun's going down and he's a little less sharp now.

"Is this home?" he says, as we settle on lawn chairs outside our door.

"No, honey. We're not going home. We're on vacation."

"Oh."

I know this trip is hard on him. The only things that tether him to the world are our house and me, and I've taken away our house. But no one, not our doctors, not our kids, not even our congressman, can convince me that this vacation is not a good idea. Hell, it's the only idea we have left.

━━━━

At first, all you see is a dense forest: sky and earth both mottled with brilliant gold and crimson and orange, a bonfire of color. It's as if fall itself has seeped into the film. Then when you look closer, deep into the blazing trees, you can see something else—the outline of the Leisure Seeker. And next to it, another camper that looks just like it, owned by our friends Jim and Dawn Jillette. The two vans are parallel to each other, their extended canopies almost touching. We used to do that to create a common area, somewhere we could move a picnic table, a place to play cards. Sometimes if it was raining, Jim and John would throw a tarp over the gap between the two canopies so we could walk freely between them.

In the next slide, the two of them are at a picnic table playing pinochle. Jim, smoking a pipe, his wire-rims wedged above his eyebrows, is frowning at the cards in his hand. Dawn, auburn hair held back with a mauve kerchief, is laughing at him. At the bottom of the frame is John's freckled hand, fanned on the gingham oilcloth.

"There's Jim!" says John, with more enthusiasm than I've seen him display this entire trip.

"And Dawn," I say.

"Old J.J."

For an instant, John sounds like his old self. J.J. was his nickname for Jim. They worked together for many years at GM, which is how we all got to be friends.

"Boy, how *is* Jim? I haven't seen him in ages."

I sigh and turn to John. "Dear. Jim died eight years ago."

"He did? Jim's dead?"

"Yes, honey. Don't you remember? We went to the funeral."
We've been through this before. John has forgotten all that he
doesn't want to remember.

"Aw, damn. Is Dawn still around?"

"I'm afraid she died a year before him."

"Aw, Christ," he says, clutching his hand over his mouth.

The fragile look on John's face makes me regret choosing
this tray of slides. I should have known better than to tell him
the truth, but I get so tired of lying to him. I just keep hoping
some of this information is going to stay put. But it never does.

I click forward. In this one, Dawn and I are walking down
a road, both carrying gorgeous bunches of brightly colored
leaves. I remember so well that we displayed them in an old
milk carton on our communal picnic table.

The next slide is just that, the bouquet of leaves on the
table, and I realize that this is the problem with photographs.
After a while, you can't remember if you're recalling the actual
memory or the memory of the photograph. Or perhaps the
photograph is the only reason you remember that moment.
(No, I refuse to believe that.)

I click the remote again. There's a picture of us all around
the campfire that John must have taken with the self-timer.
The images of all of us are dim, blurry from the long exposure,
while the fire glows bright and harsh. This last slide disturbs
me, especially with Jim and Dawn gone, so I pull out the tray.
A retina-searing whiteness is projected on the sheet hanging
from the side of the cabin, but I can't turn it off or it'll be even
harder to get in the next tray.

"Damn it, that's bright," John says.

I push in a new tray, yet it doesn't want to catch. "Just a second," I say. John used to handle the projector, now he's left it to me. He watches me fiddle with it for a while, then walks over to the table, gives the new tray a push until it clicks into place. He smirks.

"Don't be so pleased with yourself," I say. Sometimes I think his disease is more laziness than anything else.

The first slide of the tray is projected onto the sheet and around us I hear hushed chattering. I turn to see that we've attracted a crowd, gathered near a streetlight about twenty feet away. At first glance, I gasp—*hoodlums!* Then I see that they are not like the hoods of today with their baggy clothes and stocking caps and stone faces. These kids look like what we used to call juvenile delinquents. The boys wear tight white T-shirts with packs of cigarettes wedged in the sleeves, dungarees rolled at the bottom, and motorcycle boots. Their hair is greased back into carefully sculpted waterfalls and duck's asses. One of the girls is dressed in jeans and a tight blue bowling shirt and clunky black shoes. Another one wears a long felt skirt and Mary Janes, with Fire and Ice lips and an ink-black flip with bangs.

They're all covered with tattoos—arms and legs emblazoned with flames and hearts and naked ladies and skulls. Now that I focus on them a little more closely, I see that they are not really kids at all, but well into their thirties and standing there in the streetlight like walking, inky advertisements. I soon realize that they pose no threat to us. When they see me looking, a couple of them wave timidly at us and smile. They're also very fascinated with our slide show, so they can't be all bad.

Up on the screen now is a shot from our trip to Montreal for the Expo 67, yet another vacation with the Jillettes. Behind us, the sight of the Geodesic Dome has them all oohing and aahing. They're really enjoying themselves. I click to the next slide. It's one of the exhibits, I can't remember which, but the main reason John took the shot was because of the young woman in the foreground wearing a miniskirt. She has stopped to adjust something and John caught the shot as a little joke. All those mod styles had just come out and were causing quite the stir. The men certainly didn't mind. John and Jim were just about getting whiplash that trip from all the short skirts flitting around. Dawn and I put up with a lot that week.

From the Peanut Gallery behind me, I hear hoots and hollers and wolf whistles from the boys at the sight of the Canadian girl. Which proves to me that nothing has really changed. I also hear one of the girls say "cute skirt." I turn around and smile at them all.

One of the boys yells out, "Is that you, ma'am?"

"Hardly," I say back to him.

Another one steps forward. He's got the same getup on as the others, but he's the only one with a jacket on. Even though it's just a gas station grease monkey jacket, he's obviously the only one with a lick of sense. It's nippy out here tonight. He keeps walking toward us. John stands up. I look at him and shake my head.

"Everything's fine, John," I say.

"Howdy, ma'am. Hope you don't mind us enjoying your slides."

I smile. He seems very polite. I don't care what you look like as long you can show some manners. "Not at all," I say. "Enjoy yourselves. I'm Ella and that's my husband, John."

"Hello, sir," he says to John as he walks over and shakes hands. John smiles. "We're just here in town for a hot rod rally."

"That sounds nice," I say.

"Yeah, we're driving the old Route 66."

I brighten at the sound of this. "Well. That's what we're doing, too."

His eyes widen at my comment. "Really? *Cool.*" He turns to the others and yells, "They're driving 66, too!"

They laugh and nod their heads with approval. Now I know this whole thing hasn't been such a crazy idea.

Little by little, the party moves up. They seem shy, like they don't want to scare us. I can't honestly say they wouldn't have if I hadn't gotten a chance to give them a good eyeballing first.

"I'm Big Ed," says the first one.

I nod. "Yeah, I could tell by that patch over your pocket that says 'Big Ed.'"

He grins at me, smirky but sweet. "Helpful, ain't it?" Big Ed then points to the girl with the ink-black hair. "That's my wife, Missy." He then points out all the other young men and women in his group. They have names like "Gage," "Dutch," "Betty," and "Charlotta."

I say hello to them all. "You're welcome to have a seat if you want."

Big Ed looks at the others with raised brows. "Really? If you wouldn't mind, that'd be swell." Most of them park it right there on the ground. Big Ed is about to sit, then he thinks of something. "Would it be okay if I got us all some beers? We're just up the way. I'll be right back."

"Knock yourself out, Big Ed," I say.

"Care to join us?" he says, tipping an imaginary can up to his mouth.

"Sounds good."

So Big Ed picks up and runs off down the road. We are all quiet while he's gone, but within a minute I hear his boots on the asphalt again as he comes back dangling a couple of six-packs of Pabst Blue Ribbon. He throws one six-pack to the group on the ground. From the other, he pulls one off for me, then John.

Big Ed makes a big show out of cleaning off the top with his sleeve, then pops it with a little flourish, as if it were a Zippo lighter.

"Madame," he says, handing me my beer. "Sire," he says, handing John his. He's a card, this one. He then raises his can to us. "Cheers, y'all. Thanks for your hospitality."

"Thanks for yours," I say.

We all take a drink.

The kids love the slides. We polish off both six-packs as we watch all of the Expo 67 slides and I give a little running commentary about each of the exhibits we see. Over here's the

Japanese exhibit, look at that beautiful art; there's the American exhibition, have you ever seen anything so big? More miniskirts, more hoots from the boys.

"Looks like John couldn't keep his eyes off the sights," says Dutch. We all laugh. I do believe that I'm having fun. Somehow this reminds me of old times, though I've never watched slides with tattooed strangers in a hotel yard in my whole life.

A slide of the four of us in front of the Main Exposition pops up. We are all standing, smiling, before an endless row of flags from every country in the world. I tell the kids about Jim and Dawn, how we used to pal around and travel with them all the time. "We four went on quite a few trips together," I say. "Had a lot of fun."

"That's nice," says Big Ed. "It's good to go places with your friends." He turns to his wife and friends and raises his beer again. They do the same, then they drink. He then turns back to me. "Hey, so do your friends still, uh . . . ?"

He stops himself from finishing his sentence. The gang gets quiet all of a sudden.

I ignore his half question and just click to the next slide. It's Jim by himself near the GM exhibit, in front of a futuristic sedan. That's when, of course, John asks his question.

"There's ol' J.J.! How is he, Ella? I haven't seen him in ages."

I look over at him. "He's doing great, John. Just great."

The hot rod kids all smile. And so do I.

━━━━━

I don't know if it was the beer or what, but that night, John and I both sleep like logs. There is no waking and wondering, no early morning clipping of the bread bag or filing of battery ends by John; no eyes snapping open, full of the horrors, for a 4:00 A.M. crying jag by me. It's a good night. We both wake refreshed and alert.

John turns to me, opens his eyes, his old self. "Hello, dear."

"Good morning, John." He's back. "How are you?"

"I feel good," he says, yawning.

I lay my hand on his cheek. Though the years have lightened and lowered his face, it retains a kind of strength, an angularity that I have always found attractive. "You're not hungover?" I say, smiling.

He doesn't know what I'm talking about. I'm joshing, anyway. Between the two of us, we barely had three cans of beer.

"No, I'm not hungover. Do you want some breakfast?" he says to me.

I keep my hand where it is. I don't want to do anything to disturb him at this moment. "No, let's just lie here for a little while, all right?"

"Have you talked to the kids lately?"

John often asks about the kids when he is in this lucid state, as if he's been away, which he has, I suppose.

"Yes," I say. "They're doing fine. Kevin just got a promotion." That's not entirely true. They just gave him more work and a different title, but no more money.

"Good for him."

"Cindy's taking an adult education class. Basket-weaving. She's very good at it."

"That's great," he says, patting my hand, which is still resting on his cheek.

"John. Do you love me?"

He squints at me. "What the hell kind of question is that? Of course I love you." He moves closer to me and kisses me. I can smell him. He doesn't smell very good, but he still smells like my husband.

"I know," I say. "I just wanted to hear it from you. You don't say it very often anymore."

"I forget, Ella."

I forget Ella. This is what I fear most.

"I know you do, John." I lay my other hand on his face. I kiss my husband. I hold him close to me and I don't say anything more. Minutes pass, and the half night returns to his eyes.

It's time to get up.

We spend a short time on the interstate, and it's full of semitrucks that roar past us at full speed. You can sense their annoyance. We aren't going fast enough for them. As one passes us, the driver, a fat man with a camouflage hat, scowls and flips us the bird. I make a gun with my index finger and thumb and shoot it at him like Charles Bronson.

He stares at me as if I'm insane. Then he hits the gas like a bat out of hell.

We get back on 66. At Arcadia, we pass a well-known round barn, but the town itself is so drab and sad looking, we don't bother to stop. We just keep going, slow but steady till we hit Edmond, a little college town. From there we meet back up with I-44, which allows us to bypass Oklahoma City.

On the freeway, the trucks are nastier than ever. One of them comes very close to cutting us off. John has to hit the brakes, and I feel my heart jump into my throat as the weight of the van shifts forward for a moment.

Nothing happens. We keep driving. We pass a sign in front of a Knights of Columbus Council that says:

HAPPY ANNIV. DAVIE & PUNKIN 23 YRS

Good for them, I say. At Bethany, after we rejoin 66, we cross Lake Overholser on an old steel bridge, then John pulls over.

"What's wrong?" I say.

John looks at me like I'm the one losing my mind. "I have to pee."

"Oh."

He turns the engine off, then disappears into some bushes. Two minutes later, he returns to the driver's seat.

I grab our little spray bottle of hand sanitizer. "Hold out your hands."

John starts the van.

"John. You need to clean them after you pee."

"Quit riding me, Ella. Get off my back."

I spray the backs of his hands just to get his goat. He wipes them on his pants, puts it into gear, and we take off. He's getting ornery again, I can tell. We drive a little farther and I start to feel hungry.

"Let's stop for lunch, John."

"I'm not hungry."

"Well, I am." These days, I don't usually have much of an appetite, so I'd like to take advantage of it. For the first time in over forty years, I'm losing weight. Sure, I still need to go to Omar the Tent-Maker for my clothes, but he's definitely taken me down a yard or two. Too bad I had to get sick in order to lose weight. There's a diet for you. I can see it really catching on. I'll be reading all about it in the *Enquirer*—"Movie Stars Love New Cancer Diet!"

After El Reno, there's an old 1932 alignment of 66 that we could hop on, but I direct John to stay on I-44. Later, I regret my decision. I scour the countryside for restaurant billboards, but for the first time, there are none. I feel antsy and discomfortable along with my phantom hunger. Maybe I'm just anxious to get to Disneyland. I guess once I know something's going to happen, good or bad, I've never had much patience for waiting. But sometimes you just can't rush things.

"Hey look, Coney Islands! Let's stop," says John, after seeing a sign along the road.

Though I was holding out for more Oklahoma barbecue, I'm happy to see something decent to eat. In Detroit, we have Coney joints all over the city. (They've always been one of John's favorite foods. When he had to work downtown, he would sometimes sneak over to Lafayette Coney Island for two with everything before he came home. I could always tell by the onions on his breath.) But once you leave the Detroit area, you won't find them anywhere else. So it surprises me to see them here. Still, I guess the strangest thing is that both Michigan and Oklahoma have hot dogs named after a place in New York.

We down some Pepcid and head into this little shack in Hydro. It's nothing to look at from the outside, and inside, it's no better: dingy whitewashed walls, torn Naugahyde booths and chipped Formica tables. When we walk in, all the regulars turn to look at us. They scowl as if to say, "What are these rogue seniors doing in our greasy spoon?" I'd be worried if they weren't all as ancient as us.

I have to say that the Okie Coney Island looks absolutely delicious. A plate with two passes by just as we sit down. The chili looks similar to Detroit's, but they put a yellowish vinegar coleslaw on the top. We order two each, fries, and Dr Peppers (seems to be what they drink here) from a silent, burly waiter in a stained apron. Less than three minutes later, he slaps them on our table without a word.

I'm happy to report that Okie Coney dogs are indeed as delicious as they look. While we eat, an old black fellow, at least in his eighties, in a red-striped sport shirt buttoned to the top, toddles up and watches us eat for a moment. John and I exchange a glance. Not sure what to do, I smile at him and keep chewing.

MICHAEL ZADOORIAN

"Good, ain't they?" he finally says, sucking at his upper plate.

I have a little hard time understanding him, between drawl and stroke-slur, but I know what he's saying. John and I both nod yes. Our mouths are full.

"Where you all from?"

I swallow my food and wipe my face, while John keeps eating. "Detroit, Michigan," I say, with a little hesitance. No point in saying "Madison Heights, Michigan." No one's heard of it.

"Been there long?"

"All our lives."

He paws an ashy cheek as he considers this. I can't help but notice that his left eye is the color of condensed milk. "I had cousins up that way. Lived there myself for a year. Long time ago."

I set down my Coney. "Really?"

"Worked in the Packard plant there. Beautiful town."

Even though the Detroit that he's referring to is probably sixty years old, I smile again at him, genuinely touched. "Really? Well, thank you. That's so nice to hear. Usually we say we're from Detroit and everyone looks at us like we're crazy. They still call it Murder City."

He shakes his head. "Aw, folks can be so wrong-hearted. Anyway, it don't matter what they say, you stay just the same. Know what I'm talking about?"

I nod. "Yes, I do. You stay 'cause it's home."

He grins widely enough to display the pink rims of his dentures, pleased that time has taught us both the same lesson.

"That's right. Don't matter where you are, if that's where *this* is"—he splays his hand over his chest—"that's home. Sometimes you don't know why you stay, you just stay. That's *home.*"

"I couldn't agree with you more."

"Uh-huh." Both eyes close for a moment as he tips his head. "I got to go. You folks have a blessed day."

"Thank you," I say. "You take care."

He shakes both our hands and chugs slowly out the door. John looks at me, shrugs, then starts in on the remaining hot dog on my plate.

I don't know what that was all about, but it sure put me in a good mood. Back in the van, I'm not in discomfort, I'm not nauseous, my knees don't ache, I've got my wits about me, all of it. John even puts on some music—Harry James, good, jivey stuff from the '40s. For this moment, I am so happy I could cry. Granted, it has never taken much to please me, but these days, it's been a little tougher.

I think about what the man at the Coney joint said. He was right. We are the people who stay. We stay in our homes and pay them off. We stay at our jobs. We do our thirty and come home to stay even more. We stay until we are no longer able to mow our lawns and our gutters sag with saplings, until our houses look haunted to the neighborhood children. We like it where we are. I guess then the other question is: Why do we even travel?

There can be only one answer to that: we travel to appreciate home.

It doesn't matter whether you're working or taking care of children and a house, your days can't help but take on a certain sameness. As you grow older, you want that sameness, you crave it. Your kids don't understand. They're always trying to change everything, replace the very things that you find comforting and familiar, like your nicely broken-in car or the kettle that rattles when it boils. Yet the sameness is also a trap. It's part of the narrowing of your world, the tunnel vision of age. When something different happens to you, it's hard to see it as a good thing. Which means you can't always recognize a perfect moment or get yourself to a place where one can happen. Or sometimes perfect moments happen and you don't even realize it.

That is why you need to travel.

About fourteen years ago, John and I went camping at Higgins Lake. The Jillettes had planned to join us but had to cancel at the last minute, so we were on our own. It was an uneventful weekend. I woke up early Sunday morning and couldn't get back to sleep. Or maybe I had been worrying about something. (I could go on about all the time I've spent worrying in my life, but that's for another reverie, thank you.) I was sitting on a camp chair, having a cup of coffee, watching the gold light bleed upward from the earth, gradually illuminating the branches of the evergreens. I could hear the fading final stridulation of a cricket, the muffled hum of a car on a faraway road, and someone pumping water on the other side of the campground.

You're probably waiting for me to say that I saw something

miraculous, a white wolf, or some other exquisite sight that I would have never seen had I not been up so early, but I saw nothing unusual. I just sat there in front of the Leisure Seeker, knowing that this, right here, was my life. I was Ella Robina, wife of John, mother of Cindy and Kevin, grandmother of Lydia and Joseph, resident of Madison Heights, Michigan. I thought that nothing enormously bad or good had happened to me during my life. All the normal things had occurred. I had lived a completely unremarkable life. I wanted only my home, and the love and safety of those around me, nothing else. I knew there was no particular reason why I was put on this earth, but here I was and I was glad to be here, awed by the beauty of it. It was a perfect moment.

At that moment, I knew my life. Soon, I will know my death. Who knows? That could be perfect, too. But I doubt it.

"I think I'd like to take a nap," says John, some miles down the road.

"I'll get you a Pepsi, John," I say. "Let's see if we can get a few miles in before we stop for the day." Swell. Now I'm sounding like him. Truly though, we have not gone very far. Maybe one hundred and thirty miles from where we started. I would like to make it to Texas by the end of our day.

"All right."

I reach back to open the old metal Coleman cooler that we keep behind our captain's chairs to fetch John a Pepsi. The sour smell reminds me that I put a small block of Pinconning cheese in there before we left home. It's floating in water now. I dry the bottle with an old rag from under the seat. The Pepsi is warm, but that's all right. Neither of us enjoys things that are very cold or very hot. I hand it to him. He places it between his legs and tries to open it. The van swerves to one side of the road, then the other.

I grab the steering wheel. "Good Christ, John. Just a second. I'll open it."

I let go of the wheel and reach between his legs.

"Hey, watch what you're grabbing there, young lady."

I have to laugh. I smack John on the arm, twist the top off the bottle, and hand it to him.

"Lecher," I say, as he takes a big swig.

As if answering, John lets out a big belch and smiles.

"That's lovely. I hope you're proud of yourself," I say, snatching the bottle from him and taking a short sip. The pop is warm and syrupy and too fizzy, but helps my dry mouth and it settles my stomach, which is understandably starting to grumble about lunch. I hand the bottle back to John, and he takes another long pull.

It's then when I notice the flashing lights in John's side-view mirror.

"John."

"What?"

"I think the police are behind us."

He looks in the mirror, frowns. I can't tell if he's annoyed or confused.

"John, I think you should pull over."

John checks the mirror again, then his eyes return to the road. "He doesn't want us."

"I think he does, John. Pull over."

"Ella—"

"Damn it, John! *Pull over.*"

"Son of a bitch," he says as he reluctantly eases the van to the shoulder of the road. The police car does not pass us. I feel a tightness in my throat. I pray that the kids did not call the cops on us. Looking into John's mirror from my side, I see the officer walk toward us.

"John, just do what the man says." I don't need him to get in one of his contrary moods with a policeman. I want to make it to California.

"License and registration, please," says the officer, who looks about thirteen. There's a nick on his chin from shaving, which he probably does about twice a month.

"Oh, that's in my purse. Just a second," I say. He turns and peers at me.

This is unfortunate since my purse happens to be where John's gun is hidden. I grin toothily at the cop as I fumble around in my massive handbag, looking for the wallet while trying to keep a firearm out of view. The officer shifts his glance back over to John. (The advantage of being an old woman: no one expects you to be packing heat.) Finally, I find the wallet, pull out the license and registration, and hand them to the officer. All the time, John says nothing. That's good.

"Mr. Robina, the reason I stopped you was I noticed your vehicle weaving between lanes a few miles back."

I hold up the Pepsi. "Officer, that was my fault. I had given John this bottle of pop and he couldn't open it. I should have opened it before I handed it to him."

The cop gives me a pointed stare. "Ma'am, if you don't mind, I'd like Mr. Robina to answer the question."

Uh-oh. If John says something crazy, we're going to both wind up in the calaboose. Or worse, back to Detroit.

"I just was saying—"

"Ma'am, please? Mr. Robina, is that what happened?" His eyes narrow as he scans John's face.

John looks at the cop, then nods. "Yes sir, I was trying to open the thing."

"The thing?" The cop looks at him.

John clears his throat. "The thing, the, the bottle."

There is a terribly long silence as the officer scrutinizes us both. John lets out a medium loud belch, then sighs. I scowl at him. The officer leaves with John's license and registration. There is only the faint smell of Aqua Velva left in the air. From the driver's-side mirror, I can see him step into his squad car.

"What are you, nuts? You don't burp at a police officer."

John smirks at me and belches again.

It worries me what's going on in that squad car. I'm wondering if Kevin and Cindy have indeed reported us. Both had decided a few months back (at one of their "What are we going to do about Mom and Dad?" meetings, no doubt) that John should no longer own a valid driver's license. Kevin had already tried to disable our old Impala, but he underestimated us. John opened the hood, I spotted the distributor wire that Kevin had yanked, and we had the car running again in nothing flat. Even beyond the teen years, parents still have to prove to their children that they are not as stupid as they think. After that, Kevin and Cindy both shut up for a while, until a few weeks ago. That's when the "Dad shouldn't be driving" talks started anew. Except this time, we took it on the lam.

Right about now, John starts up the Leisure Seeker again. He is about to put it into gear when I reach over and turn the key off. I pull it out of the ignition.

I hiss at him. "Are you off your rocker?"

"Give me those fucking keys," he says.

"What do you think? You're going to lose him in this monster? We're going to have a high-speed chase like they do on the news in Detroit?"

John looks at me with such hatred that it breaks my heart. I think, *He's finally going to belt me after all these years.* Then I'm going to have to kill him. The old John knows that I would do that, but maybe not this one. I ball up the keys in my fist, ready for anything. Then I look in the side mirror again.

"Shut up, he's coming back," I say, watching the cop get larger in the mirror. He steps up to the side of the van.

"Thought you were going to take off on me for a minute," he says, smiling. He hands John back his license and registration. "You're all set. Please be more careful. Stay in your lane and proceed at the posted limits, all right?"

I smile again at the officer, playing up the *sweet old dear* routine for all it's worth. "We certainly will, Officer. Thanks so much. Have a nice day!"

I watch him get back in his squad car and drive away. I'm cold and my body feels absolutely limp. I'm so relieved that there wasn't an APB out on us, or whatever they used to do on *Adam-12*.

"Where are the keys?" says John, checking all the cup holders and niches on the dash. He could be looking for quite some time. He has the inside of this van so glopped up with gadgets and magnetic contraptions and compasses and dispensers, it's amazing that we can even move in here.

I drop the keys firmly in his lap.

"Ow!" yelps John, cupping his crotch.

"Let's go, Barney Oldfield."

No sooner do we get going than we decide to stop again. I see a sign for the Route 66 Museum in Clinton. I am torn between wanting to get to Texas and seeing this museum. As we approach it, I decide that we need a rest after our little run-in with the fuzz.

"We're going to have a look at this museum," I say to John, wondering if he's going to give me any lip.

"Oh. Okay. Looks good."

It does look good. It's modern and sleek, with lots of glass block, right in the middle of all this flatness. There's a bright red convertible in the front display window.

We park the van and John helps me get out. I bring my cane. I'm not feeling tip-top, but decide to ignore it. I haven't taken my meds this afternoon. Too busy gobbling down Coneys and harassing the authorities, I guess.

On our way in, we pass a monument to the lassoin' buffoon, Will Rogers. I've already had a bellyful of that knucklehead and we're not even halfway to California.

I'll give them this. There's a lot of stuff at this museum. *Too* much. Every square inch of the place is filled. Antique cars, motorcycles, a dust bowl jalopy with water bags slung over the bumpers, giant photographs, rusty license plates, old billboards, not to mention dinging gas pumps, blinking traffic lights, buzzing neon hotel signs; as well as a Volkswagen hippie van spray-painted in all kinds of crazy colors that hurt my eyes to even look at.

Before long, we're both walking around in a daze, overstimulated by all the noise and colors and lights.

"I don't feel so good," says John.

"Me, neither. Let's get out of here."

This is the first museum to ever give us a headache.

Once we're back on the road, I start to feel better. I do, however, notice what must be the sixth half-filled plastic bottle of pee that I've seen along the side of the road. I swear they're all over the place in Oklahoma. What is wrong with these people? It alarms me to think about all these Okies urinating while they drive. Keep your hands on the wheel, I say!

———

Before Erick, we pass a sign:

ROGER MILLER MEMORIAL HIGHWAY

"That can't be the guy who sang 'King of the Road,' can it?" I say.

John starts crooning to me. "*Trai*-lers for sale . . ." He taps his fingers on the steering wheel as he sings.

He can't remember my goddamn name, but he can remember a stupid song from forty years ago. When I see the sign for the Roger Miller Museum, sure enough there's a big "King of the Road" banner. He must be from around here. Good Lord. Oh well, at least it's not Will Rogers.

I pull down the visor and examine myself in the mirror. There are long strands of hair—dirty hair, I'm ashamed to admit—all blown and scattered about my head. As much as I gripe about John's hygiene, you think I'd be more conscious of my own. I pull the elastic band from my hair and attempt to gather the strands back into the pigtail. I extend my neck, try to get a glimpse of the woman I once was, but she is nowhere to be found. I take off my glasses, hoping the blur will help, but I only end up examining the circles beneath my eyes that have grown darker and deeper over the past days. How can someone manage to look gaunt while maintaining a double chin, I ask you?

"I look like the wreck of the *Hesperus*," I mutter.

John turns and says, "I think you look beautiful."

I look at my husband. It's been ages since he's said anything like that to me. I think about how I used to crave his compliments, how I used to believe them, how they used to keep me from cringing when I looked in the mirror.

"You're full of it," I say, playing a game of ours from long ago.

"That's true, but I still think you're beautiful."

Damn this man. Damn him to hell for still loving me, even now.

We approach the town of Texola. Just off the road, we see ancient cars parked along property lines, rusting hulks with FOR SALE signs fading in the sun, as if they are waiting for some classic car collector to come rescue them from the junkyard. The grass is burnt brown. The buildings are crumbling. There's no one in sight.

Seven

TEXAS

The late afternoon sun angles in hard on us. Maybe it's just my imagination, but it's hotter here. I guess even though it's fall, it's still Texas. We put on our big sungoggles, roll up the windows, and turn on the air-conditioning for the first time. Unfortunately, it doesn't take long to realize that the air-conditioning doesn't work very well. John probably hasn't had it recharged in years. I turn it up all the way, but the air it blows is mossy and acrid, just barely cool.

The other thing I realize is something I already knew. The exhaust problem that Kevin mentioned was never fixed. Consequently, rolling up the windows is not a good idea. Tepid air is not the only thing coming from the vents; there is also a mist of exhaust pouring in. Within minutes, we're both yawning like crazy. I turn off the AC, roll the windows down, and immediately feel better. John wakes up as well.

Even still, I fear I may have pushed him too hard today. He's talking to himself under his breath, like he's forgotten I'm here. I'm hoping we'll find somewhere to stay in Shamrock, which is the next big town. I check my books for campgrounds and am relieved to find one right on West I-40, parallel to 66.

After passing a fancy 1930s art deco gas station called the "U Drop Inn," we arrive at the campground. I have John park near the check-in station. He turns off the engine.

"Is this home?"

He's tired and disoriented. "No, John. I'm going to go check us in. You don't need to come." I grab my cane and purse, then slowly lower myself from the van. I'm feeling shaky, so I try to be extra careful. Halfway to the office, I think of something so I turn and head back to the van.

"Oh John, could you give me the keys?" I say sweetly. Without discussing the matter, John hands them over.

When I stump into the office with my cane, the old man behind the counter just stands there staring at me as I walk up. He frowns and snorts, as if to say "This one's ready for the glue factory."

I should tell you, I have no tolerance for staring, particularly with people my age, who love to act like the whole world is their television. It grinds me, especially since most of us spent our best years telling our children that it's impolite to stare. I don't know where this one gets off. He's no prize, believe you me: greasy fishing hat, a forehead mole you could hang a hat on, and a face that looks like he's been sniffing Limburger cheese for the past dozen or so years.

I stare right back at him.

"Hello," he finally says, blinking. I guess I win.

"Good afternoon," I say, after a long pause. "We need a campsite for the night."

"All right," he says, a low Texas growl to his voice. "We're pretty open today. Anywhere in particular?"

From what I could see, all the spaces look the same, a few trees here and there, but mostly flat and dry.

"Near a shower facility would be good," I tell him. I give him a twenty. He fills out a card, tears off part of that, and hands it to me with my change. Then he starts eyeballing me again.

"Pardon me? Is there something wrong?" I say to him, huffy now, raring for it.

"Are you ready?" he says, his voice gentler now.

"Ready for what?" My hand tightens on the grip of my cane.

"Ready to accept Jesus as your personal savior?"

"Oh, for Christ's sake," I say, too tired for this. "Maybe some other time."

"Never too late, you know."

"I know," I say, making a break for the door, fast as I can haul myself.

Once we find the site and I get John out of the van, he's a little better. He can still set up the electricity. I watch him

111

closely because I'm not sure when I'll have to do it. If he gets worse as the trip wears on, it'll be up to me. That is, unless I accept Jesus as my personal savior, then maybe He can do it.

We are so pooped by the time we get settled that we both just conk out—John on the bed, me at the table after taking my meds. (I'm more comfortable sitting up sleeping these days. Lying down seems more of a commitment, fraught with responsibilities and forebodings.) It's only 4:15 but it feels like it's about 10:00 P.M. I can hardly keep my eyes open, but I do remember to turn a light on so we don't wake up in the dark like last time.

When I wake up, the air in the van is hot and still. I'm not in the dark, but I am alone. John is gone. I grab my cane, get myself up, and head outside, but he's not sitting at the picnic table. He's nowhere around. I start to panic.

A few trailers are parked nearby, yet no one seems to be around. We're only a short ways from the restrooms, so I head over there.

"Is anyone in there?" I yell at the men's room entrance. Nothing. I hobble on in. The place is deserted. Just concrete and wads of paper towel and the sour tang of urine.

I head for the office, but it's a good half block away. Along the way, every bad thing that could happen runs through my head—John walking along the highway getting hit by a car; John lost in the woods never to be found again; disoriented John picked up by strangers.

I shuffle along until I get to the check-in office. I am already exhausted and ready to weep. Luckily, the Jesus fellow is behind the counter and while he does give me the stare again, he is at least civil.

"Hello," he says. His low-pitched voice now gives me the heebie-jeebies, but I have to be nice because he's my only chance.

"I was wondering if you've seen my husband pass by? He's about six feet tall, a little hunched over, with a green shirt and a tan golf cap on?"

Old Jesus just looks at me for a second. I think he's going to give me his spiel again, but he doesn't. "A man that fits that description passed by a short while ago."

"He did? How long?"

"Maybe fifteen minutes ago," he says, his voice gaining a little speed now, sounding more human to me, which gives me a teaspoon of hope.

"That's him. Look, could you help me? He occasionally has little spells where he doesn't know where he is. I'm afraid he's going to get lost or hurt."

"Should I call the police?"

"Let's not do that yet." I've had enough of the police for today. "Do you have a car? Maybe we could just drive around. He's probably not far away."

Old Jesus looks highly alarmed at this idea.

"I'm sure it won't take long," I say.

"I can't leave my post here. Can't you just drive your camper?"

113

I'm really starting to get scared now. "I can't drive that thing. Please. I wouldn't ask if it wasn't important."

He thinks for a moment, and it looks like hard work for him. I want to smack him one, but he's got to be the one to help me. There's really no one else around. He's silent for a good thirty seconds.

"*Please,*" I say.

Finally, he speaks. "I could see if Terry could drive you. He's our groundskeeper. He's got a truck."

"That would be fine. Please hurry."

Another bout of hard thinking. Finally, he picks up a phone and methodically punches in the numbers. Meanwhile, I'm picturing John walking around in traffic, horns blaring. I don't think he'd be crazy enough to do that, but I just don't know anymore. I watch Old Jesus' face as he listens to the phone ring. It's like staring through a screen door at an empty house. I hear someone answer at the other end.

"Terry? It's Chet at the office. There's a lady here who needs some help. We were wondering—"

He stops for a moment and listens. I can tell Terry is not cooperating.

"I know. She says she needs help. I can't leave the desk."

More talking. Finally, I pipe up. "May I speak to him, please?"

Chet looks appalled at the idea. The phone has suddenly become like the desk. He can't abandon it. Finally, I just grab it from him. "Hello, Terry?"

There is a long pause and I think I've stumbled onto a cult

of dim-witted Christians, but when Terry speaks, he sounds fairly normal. "Who is this?" he says.

"Terry, I'm the woman who needs the help. This is an emergency. My husband is lost, and I'm afraid he's going to be hurt. He has spells where he's disoriented. Could you just please come here? I just need you to drive me around the area. I'll be happy to pay for your gas and time."

"I'll be there in a minute or so, ma'am."

Sure enough, within a minute, a little maroon pickup truck with gold hubcaps rumbles up to the door of the office and honks. I hear a deep *whomp-whomp* rhythm vibrating from the radio.

"Thank you very much," I say to Chet, who is now gazing off into space. Actually, I'm hoping he'll say something spiritually encouraging right now because I could use it, but he obviously doesn't have it in him. He just turns and stares at me.

The music cuts off. I head outside expecting to have to raise myself into the passenger side of the pickup truck, but it is actually quite low. As I twist myself in, I realize I'm getting in a truck with a complete stranger. I look at who's driving and decide that this is probably where most abduction witness testimonies begin. *She never should've gotten into that truck with that man.*

Terry, I should say here, scares the living hell out of me. He's around twenty years old, the last remnants of acne across his jutting cheekbones, with long dishwater brown hair streaming out from under a black watch cap that looks like it hasn't been washed in a month of Sundays. His T-shirt is black, his baggy pants are black (with chains hanging from them), the finger-less glove on his right hand is black—everything he's wearing is black. The front of his shirt has a greenish photograph of a downright evil-looking man with long puke-colored hair and a powder white face with a bloody X scratched into his fore-head. Underneath the picture, it says:

100% HARDCORE
FLESH-EATING
BLOOD-DRINKING
LIFE-SUCKING
ZOMBIE
HELLBILLY!

Yet once I get past all that, I give him a better look and I can't help but be reminded of my Kevin when he was that age: trying so hard to look tough, but betrayed by the gentleness of his eyes. The truck smells of cigarettes and perspiration and the artificial strawberry scent from the flaming pentagram air freshener hanging from the rearview mirror.

"I'm Terry," he says, holding out his gloved hand to shake mine. I notice his other hand has a word tattooed just below the knuckles. It says "O F F !"

"Ella." I shake his hand and try to smile. This is no time for me to be choosy. If Satan has decided to help me as opposed to what was back at the office, then so be it. Though I think both would be well advised to reconsider their role models.

"You're sweating," Terry says to me. It's a strange thing to say.

I touch my forehead and see that he is absolutely correct about this. "I'm worried about my husband."

"Sounds like Chester in there wasn't so much help," he says, pulling at the random straggly hairs on his chin.

I look at this child. "No, I can't say that he was," I say sharply. "Are you going to be any help?"

He purses his lips together in an exaggerated manner and nods. "We'll find the old dude," he says, as we pull out onto I-40.

Like I haven't seen enough of this goddamned road today. A half mile up, we see someone in a beige jacket walking on the shoulder.

"Is that him?" says Terry, pointing.

"No," I say. "John's got a green shirt on." I can see through the knuckle holes on his glove that Terry has something or other tattooed on his right hand. It occurs to me that if Terry ever wants to get another job, having things tattooed on his hands is not going to be considered an asset by most employers.

I sigh and I'm afraid I do it a bit louder than I mean to. Terry looks at me, and I'm surprised by the concern in his voice. "We'll find him. I'm telling you. It's okay."

"Thank you."

It's quiet in the truck for a minute. Terry turns to me and says, "My grammy had it, too."

"Had what?"

"I don't know," he says, half shrugging. "Whatever they call it. That dude's name. The disease. She used to go walking around the neighborhood. She had to go into a nursing home. She was dead in a year." Terry softly exhales. "She was the only one in my family worth a shit." He looks into the rearview mirror, then at me. "Sorry."

This young man obviously has me mixed up with some old lady who doesn't cuss like a longshoreman. I look at him and try to smile. "It's all right," I say. "It's an emergency."

I scan the side of the road. There are a few little stores scattered here and there. He could be at any of them. We pass an old Standard gas station, then a bright-painted sign shaped like an ice cream cone that says DAIRY IGLOO. Off the road, a big penguin waves to us from the side of a white-painted cinder-block hut. People are gathered around it, either waiting in line or eating ice cream cones. A little farther from the place is a cluster of picnic tables. That's where I see John. He's sitting and eating a chocolate frozen custard.

"There he is!" I yell. "Pull over."

"Where?"

I point frantically to the right. "The ice cream place. Over there!"

Terry steers us into the parking lot and we pull up almost right next to John. He looks at me. I'm sure he doesn't recognize me since I'm in this strange little truck. I open the door and pull myself out.

"John." I walk as fast as I can over to him and throw my arms around him. "Jesus Christ, John." I'm ready to start bawling right there at the Dairy Igloo. I squeeze John as hard as I can.

"Ella?"

I hold on to him for dear life. "I need you right now. I need you to stay with me. We don't have that much time, John."

"I don't know what you mean, Ella."

I pull back from him and look him straight in the eyes. "Honey, you scared the dickens out of me." People from the front of the Dairy Igloo are starting to look over at us now. I lower my voice.

John licks at his cone, looks at me like this is no big thing at all. "I just decided to go for a walk."

"Oh, you just decided to go for a walk?" I am trying not to get mad now. I don't want to yell in front of all these people. "John, do you have any idea how to get back from here? Do you know where you're going at all?"

He points back the way we came. "Back that way."

"Give me that thing," I say, snatching the ice cream cone from his hand. I give it a lick. It's sweet and cold and tastes wonderful and it makes me start to cry. I sit down on the bench and can't seem to stop crying.

John puts his arm around me, gathers me close. "What are you crying for?"

"Nothing," I say.

Just then, Terry steps from his truck and approaches us.

"Who's this?" says John, suspiciously.

It takes me a moment to compose myself. I hand John back his ice cream cone. Snuffling, I pull a tissue from my sleeve, blow my nose. "This is Terry, the young man who helped me find you."

"Hmph," grunts John. He gives Terry a look like he might give a convicted felon, which Terry may be, but I doubt it.

I blow my nose again. "Terry," I say, my voice cracking, "may we buy you an ice cream?"

He nods timidly. I pull out a twenty from my purse. "Could you get me one, too?"

Terry flashes a sad smile at me, far too sad for someone his age. I sit there next to John, my arm around his waist.

A few minutes later, Terry comes back with two chocolate-vanilla swirls and a handful of my change. I take my cone, then close his hand around the bills and coins.

The glove is off now and I can finally read the tattoo on his right hand. It says "F U C K." Now I understand what's on his other hand.

I know just what he means.

That night, we go to bed early—no cocktail hour, no slide show, no TV. I make us some grilled cheese sandwiches and tomato soup, then give us each a Valium. I hate those things, but tonight I need to be sure that John is going to sleep. I force myself to stay up until I can hear him snoring, then I lock the door and bolt it shut. I lie down next to him so he'll have a harder time getting up without waking me up. Tonight I'm taking no chances.

When I finally allow myself to relax, I'm not tired anymore. I start thinking about the kids. I meant to give Cindy a call today, but forgot in all the excitement. I think about Cindy's job at Meijer's Thrifty Acres and how hard she works, how these big stores take advantage of their employees. So many extra hours and no extra pay. I think of how tired I know she is, getting up at 4:00 A.M. every day. Then I start thinking about my old job, the one I had when we first got married. It was just a salesgirl position at Winkleman's, but I liked being around people all day, loved the fashions, and we sure needed the money. When Cindy came along, I quit, thinking that some day I'd go back, but it never happened. John wouldn't have gotten on his high horse about having a "working wife," but it was assumed that I would be there to raise the kids and that was fine with me.

As the years passed, I would think about going back to work now and then, but there was always plenty to do around the house. I remember seriously considering it one day when Kevin was a toddler and being an absolute terror around the house. (He would eat everything in sight—bugs, cleaning supplies, plants, medicine—whatever it was, it went into his mouth. The poison control center knew me by name.) That child ran me ragged. And no sooner would I get him settled than Cindy would come home from school to get him all riled up again. Having a job would have been nice around that time.

I never meant to bury my talent in a napkin. The fact was, I never really knew if I had a talent for anything, except for being a wife and mother. I do know I loved doing the displays at the store. Sometimes I'd even get a chance to do a window. I always had a flair for that sort of thing—putting colors together, fabrics, textures, all of it. At the store, everyone was always pleased with what I did. Mr. Biliti, the manager, a thin man with a moustache and a little dandruff problem, always told me what a good job I had done. I remember his disappointment when I announced I was pregnant. He smiled and congratulated me, and immediately began to ignore me. Before long, it was like I didn't even exist. He knew what would happen. He worked in a women's store, after all.

To be truthful, I rarely thought about any of them after I left. I was happy to be where I was, happy to be a mom, with a house and a husband. And John was a good husband. We made a good home for our children. We both came from homes ruled by tyrants and adulterers and martyrs, where we lived with constant arguments and beatings, so we decided that whatever our parents did, we would do the opposite. All in all, it was a pretty good plan.

We always looked at our marriage as a team. Neither one of us is more important. I never waited on John hand and foot, like some women. If he wanted a sandwich, he could jolly well get up and make it himself. We have always been very modern that way. This is marriage, not indentured servitude.

Which is why his remarks lately about the house being "his house" and everything else being purchased with "his money" have hurt me so. I know it's the disease talking, that people like him start getting that way about money and such. Still, it used to be that he would never say anything like that to me.

I'm not even sure he remembers that we've had two houses, one in Detroit before the one in Madison Heights. We, like most everyone else like us, moved out of Detroit a few years after the '67 riots. It broke my heart to leave that house. We lived there almost twenty years. But things changed, neighborhoods changed. White people were scared, moving out by the swarm. There was blockbusting, real estate people knocking on your door telling you that "they" were moving into your neighborhood, spreading stories about break-ins and robberies. All that talk. That talk made me scared to walk around my own neighborhood.

When I grew up, we lived on Tillman Street in the city, in an area that was very poor. Black folks lived on our block with us and it didn't matter then. We had everyone on our street—Bulgarians; Irish; Czech; lots of Poles; a Jew; some French (the Millers, who were all thieves); and a black man, Mr. Williams, who lived with his daughter, Zula Mae; even a mixed-race couple, a white woman and a black man. It didn't matter because we were all poor. We all owned nothing and all lived peacefully.

Everything just seemed to fall apart after the riots. Coleman Young was elected mayor and made it pretty clear that he didn't like white people. He told us all to hit Eight Mile Road and keep going. Before long, everyone I knew, my sisters and brother, all our neighbors and friends, moved out of Detroit.

Except us. Again, I lived down the street from black folks and I told myself that it wouldn't matter, but it was different this time. We were made to feel that Detroit was their city now. I guess we weren't so used to being the minority. I didn't want to leave my home. I loved that house. But we left it.

It still breaks my heart to see what happened. So many slums and abandoned buildings. Michigan Central Station, the National Theatre, J.L. Hudson's, the Statler, the Michigan Theatre, all destroyed or left to rot. Now I hear white people are starting to move back into the city. Buildings are being renovated. There are new condos and developments and office complexes. Things are changing again. I don't know what to think. What is white has become black, what is black becomes white. And these days, these lingering days, John and I live in between, in a grayworld where nothing seems really real, and the places that were once so important to us are forever gone.

I have to go to the bathroom, but I don't want to get up yet. I just want to lie here for a few moments more. I wonder what happened to all of them at Winkleman's. Most of them were older than me. They are dead now, I'm sure of that, just like almost all of our friends, the ones who moved with us from the city to the suburbs. The Jillettes, the Nears, the Meekers, the Turnblooms, almost all gone, except for a straggling widow here and there.

You worry about parents, siblings, spouses dying, yet no

one prepares you for your friends dying. Every time you flip through your address book, you are reminded of it—*she's gone, he's gone, they're both gone*. Names and numbers and addresses scratched out. Page after page of gone, gone, gone. The sense of loss that you feel isn't just for the person. It is the death of your youth, the death of fun, of warm conversations and too many drinks, of long weekends, of shared pains and victories and jealousies, of secrets that you couldn't tell anyone else, of memories that only you two shared. It's the death of your monthly pinochle game.

Know this: even if you're like us and still doddering around above ground, someone out there from your past is probably pretty sure that you're dead by now.

At 4:23 A.M., I wake from my usual flimsy slumber to find John standing over me, lips knitted over teeth, forehead veined with rage. I think I've mentioned that sometimes he isn't able to distinguish his dreams from reality. Sometimes he wakes up and doesn't know where he is or who he is. And he's mad as Hades about it.

"John, what's wrong?" I say, sitting up in bed.

He glares at me, mouth open, his breath ragged and phlegmy.

"John, what is *wrong*?" I say, noticing something glinting in his hand. I thought, this is it, he's finally gone round the bend. "What do you have there? What are you thinking? You were just having a dream."

"No, I'm not," he growls. "I'm awake. Where are we? This isn't home. Where have you taken me?"

"John. This is our camper. We're on vacation, remember? I'm your wife. I'm Ella."

"You're not Ella." He barks it at me, between clenched teeth.

"Of course I'm Ella. I know who I am. I'm your wife, I'm Ella."

His eyes soften a little as if what I'm saying is starting to make some sense to him. "What are you holding there, John?"

He holds out his hand so I can see what he's got. It's a knife.

A butter knife.

"Give me that, you horse's ass." I'm ready to smack him one by now.

When I call him that, it seems to prove to him that I am indeed Ella. He hands me the knife and I feel something on the blade, something sticky.

"Were you making a sandwich, John?" I take a closer look at him.

"No."

"Then how come there's peanut butter on your face?" I take a tissue from my pocket, wet it at my mouth, and wipe his upper lip.

"I don't know."

"Good Christ. Come to bed, John."

It's not the first time this has happened. The last time at

home, he just shook me awake clutching the neckline of my nightgown. The time before that was the scary one. He was holding a claw hammer and he kept banging his nightstand, demanding to know where he was.

Right after that, I started having a hard time sleeping. It's not just from being afraid of my husband. It doesn't upset me to think about dying. What upsets me is the idea of John being alone after his spell passes. The idea of one of us without the other.

The morning sky is annoyingly blue. John wakes up quiet but chipper, whereas I am grouchy as hell. We have toast and tea and oatmeal, meds, then pack up and move out. Getting back on the road is a welcome relief. I decide to forget about yesterday and concentrate on what's ahead. We have a long pass through the panhandle of Texas ahead of us, at least one hundred sixty miles.

The landscape is flat and uncheering—scalded rock and cracked earth, scabbed with wiry bush. Just to be on the safe side, I make John stop to fill up the Leisure Seeker. After I put in our credit card and get John started, I visit the ladies' room, then buy us snacks and two big bottles of water. (I hate spending money on water, but it makes me feel better to have them.)

John is still filling up when I get back. I think he hasn't been pressing the nozzle trigger beyond a trickle. He smiles at me as I walk toward the van. He's wearing a big golf hat with the American flag on it that he must have found somewhere.

"We all set, El?" he says through the open window after I climb in.

"Set as we're gonna be," I say, surprised to hear that name again. It's been years since John has called me "El." These are the things the disease steals from you, one by one, the little familiars, the details that make that person feel like home. These are also the things that this trip is stirring back up to the surface again. I like that.

The nozzle snaps itself off. John hooks it back on the pump, then opens the van door. Our credit receipt curls out from a slot on the pump, quivers in the wind, then flits away. We are not worrying about such things. John settles in his captain's chair, beams at me, gives my knee a squeeze.

"Hey lover," he says, looking pleased, though most of what he's feeling there is fat and titanium. I don't mind telling you that just then, my heart soars.

I smile back, in a better mood now, and glad to see my old man. "Someone's full of piss and vinegar today," I say.

He pats my knee and starts the van. We need this after yesterday.

We decide to forgo the "Devil's Rope" Barbed Wire Museum in McLean because it sounds like it could be the silliest museum in the world. Not long after, we pass a little old-fashioned Phillips 66 gas station with orange pumps and a milk-bottle-shaped chimney. Like a lot of the things that people have restored on this road, it doesn't actually work, but it looks good.

The miles pass easily. It is hot and clear and arid, but

not uncomfortable with the windows open. The advantage of traveling in fall. Route 66 is the frontage road alongside the freeway, uncrowded as we pass through towns with names like Lela and Alanreed. You could call these places sleepy, although *comatose* may be more like it. A sign off the freeway:

RATTLESNAKES EXIT NOW

Yet at the Reptile Ranch, there is nothing left but rubble. I almost want to have John pull over for a closer look, but instead I direct us onto I-40 to avoid the dirt road section of 66 coming up, what's left of the Jericho Gap. Anyway, it feels so good to be moving that I wouldn't want to ruin our momentum by lollygagging. I also don't want to do anything that will make John any different than he is right now. He is downright chatty.

"Ella, remember when we went to Colorado that time? Where were we when we woke up and there were all those sheep all around us? God, that was something."

I turn to John, amazed. He hasn't recalled anything like this for a long time, but I'm not complaining. "It was Vail," I say. "When we went out west in '69."

"That's right!" he says, nodding with his whole body.

"That was so strange," I say. "We woke up early and I happened to look outside. The sun had just come up and all these sheep just appeared."

John pushes back his glasses with his index finger and

nods again. "That man was herding them through the camp-ground. We were right next to that hillside and they stopped and grazed all around us. I don't know how he managed all of them."

"Did he have a dog?" I can't believe that I'm asking John about something that happened decades ago.

"I don't think so." As he speaks, John stares at the road before us as if he's watching the scene unfold right there. "I remember how that felt. It was like time slowed down when those sheep surrounded us. Everything got so still while they grazed. They weren't even that noisy. I remember feeling like we were trapped in the camper. But it was all right. We were just surrounded by sheep."

"That's what I like about vacation," I say, gazing out my window at the brownish puffs of undergrowth dotting the roadside.

"Sheep?"

"Everything slows down. You have all these experiences in a short period. You can't remember what day it is. Time slows like a dream."

John looks stymied by what I just said. Or maybe he didn't even hear me. Just as well, since I've probably just described his usual state of mind.

"Remember how scared Kevin was?" he says. "Poor kid had never seen so many sheep. Not even at the State Fair. I had to tell him that everything was okay. That sheep are nice and you don't have to be afraid of them."

"Good grief, John." He's giving me details that even I forgot and I've got a memory to match my girth. I put my hand on his forearm, run my nails through the snowy hair.

"What?"

"Nothing. Nothing at all."

There are no perfect moments. Not anymore. I realize this now because this day, this brief moment where I have my John back, is the same time that I suddenly feel pressure in my body, an intense, gut-crushing discomfort like no discomfort I've experienced so far. I remove my quivering hand from John's arm, glad that I didn't sink my nails into the flesh when the first wave hit. I fumble around in my purse for my little blue pills. I look and look, my purse is full of pill bottles, just not the right ones. I find tubes of lipstick, wads of Kleenex, half-sticks of Doublemint, and John's gun (so very heavy, but I am scared to leave it anywhere else), but no little blue pills. Finally, I locate the vial. Hands shaking like a dope fiend, I wash two down with the emergency water. It's going to be a while, I know, before I feel any relief. I need distraction.

"Talk to me, John," I say, wincing, but trying to keep my voice as normal as possible.

"About what?"

"Anything. I don't care. Tell me what you remember."

"About what?"

"About us. About our marriage. Tell me something."

John looks at me, confused at first, as if on the verge of forgetting the question. Then he blurts it out: "How you looked when we got married. I remember how red your cheeks were. You weren't wearing any rouge, but your cheeks were so red.

I kept thinking you were running a fever. I remember kissing you on the steps of St. Cecilia, touching your face and feeling how warm it was and thinking that I wanted to feel that warmth against my face."

I wince. "I remember you doing that. Your face was nice and cool. I was so keyed up that day. I just wanted us to be married."

John laughs and smiles at me. I hope my grimace passes for a smile.

"Tell me something else you remember, John. Hurry."

"I remember after Kevin was born. I went home after you were all settled in for the night and the baby was okay. Cindy was staying with your sister and I was alone at home and I couldn't stop crying."

"Why were you crying, John?"

"I don't remember. I think I was happy. I remember being ashamed for crying so much."

"There was nothing to be ashamed of, sweetie."

"I guess not."

I close my fingers around the armrests of my captain's chair and ride it out. "You used to get so mad at Kevin for crying all the time."

"I didn't want him to get picked on at school for being a crybaby."

"He still was anyway." I can't laugh or smile right now, but I want to.

John doesn't say anything. A car passes us on the left spewing exhaust fumes. The smell of the fumes makes me nauseous. I almost think I'm going to upchuck, but I roll down my window farther and it helps.

"What do you remember about vacation, John?"

He thinks for a moment. A ragged jolt of discomfort shoots through me. *"John."*

"Fire. The fires we would have. The campfire smell on my clothes the next morning when I would get up and put the same sweatshirt on. I liked that smell. By the end of the day driving, it would be gone and I wanted it back."

"Maybe we'll have a fire tonight."

"All right."

We pass the town of Groom and I can see the "Leaning Tower of Texas," as the guidebooks call it. It's a water tower lurched way over to one side.

"Are you all right?" John asks.

"I'm fine," I lie. Another car rockets past us.

"What's his hurry?" says John, irked. This has happened a lot this trip, people ticked off at the oldsters driving so slowly, but this is the first time John has noticed. I worry that we did the same thing when we were young, our impatient travels, going too fast to get somewhere, then hurrying back home. I think of the map in our basement with the tape lines webbed over the country, all those vacations, how fast this all went by. I think of the Joads trudging through the Jericho Gap, their truck being sucked into the earth. Then a quicksilver warmth starts spreading through my bones. My head loosens on my shoulders, and I can breathe again. Outside my window, I see a grain elevator in a field, its silos like fingers clutching at the sky.

I have achieved comfort.

"Howdy, partners!" says Jeanette, our pretty, perky waitress, all gussied up like a cowgirl, still young enough not to be completely beaten down by grueling waitress work. "Welcome to the Big Texan Steak Ranch!"

"Howdy, little lady," John says back, tipping his golf hat to her. He's still doing well and it's brought out the flirt in him.

Jeanette laughs much too long and much too loudly at this. "Well, aren't you two just the cutest thing?"

I nod and smile. Jeanette has no idea that the cute little old lady she's waiting on is high as a kite on the dope. Maybe I took a little too much. My head is humming. My body feels liquid and electric. The discomfort is gone, but so am I. I'm lucky I made it to the table.

The Big Texan Steak Ranch is a gaudy place that looked like great fun from the outside—a giant cowboy and his giant cow, right next to a giant ranch house. John was so excited when he saw the place, I couldn't disappoint him. (In case you haven't noticed, I am a sucker for the jumbo tourist attractions. I still get a thrill passing the enormous Ferris wheel–sized Uniroyal tire on I-94 back in Detroit. And I used to love that colossal Paul Bunyan we had up north in Michigan. I have a photo somewhere of Cindy and myself when she

134

was just five or six, standing next to Babe the Blue Ox. We are looking up and waving at John taking the picture from high above us in Paul Bunyan's head.) Anyway, now that we're inside the Big Texan, it looks more like an Old West bordello than a ranch house. On top of that, a big hunk of meat doesn't exactly sound appetizing to me right now.

"All right, you cuties. What'll y'all have?" squeaks Jeanette.

"I want a hamburger," says John. No newsflash there.

"Is the eight-ounce chopped steak all right?"

I nod at Jeanette. "That's fine for him. Well done, please."

"You also get a salad and two sides, sir."

John looks a tad bewildered, so I perk up, though I'm loopy myself. "Uhhh, Thousand Island dressing?" I say, stalling, as I scan the giant, crazy, cartoon-filled menu. "Mac and cheese. Fried okra."

"Okay. And you, ma'am?" asks Jeanette, head cocked.

"I'll just have a glass of sweet tea, please."

Jeanette pouts theatrically at my answer. "You sure? Don't forget we've got our special Big Texan seventy-two-ounce steak. Four and a half pounds! It's free if you can eat it all in an hour!"

I stare at her blankly. "Um. No, I don't think I'll be having that today, thanks."

"We've had a sixty-nine-year-old meemaw eat one," Jeanette proclaims proudly.

"Is that so?" I say. "Well, this meemaw just wants sweet tea."

"Okay! I'll be right back with your bread and butter!" Jeanette leaves, and I am relieved. It's a strain being around all that enthusiasm.

John looks at me, concerned. "Are you all right, honey?"

"I'm fine. Just a little queasy."

"Are you sick?"

This might be an appropriate time to mention that John doesn't really know that I'm ill. I mean, he knows that the kids take me to the doctor. (We tape notes all through the house—MOM AT DOCTOR. BACK IN TWO HOURS!—so he doesn't panic when he realizes I'm not there.) But he doesn't know why. He wouldn't be able to retain the information, anyway. When Cindy told John about her divorce, he kept forgetting. Every time he saw her, he'd ask, "Where's Hank?"

She'd say something like, "I don't know, Dad. We're divorced. He just comes by to pick up the kids."

"Divorced!" John would say. "What? You're not divorced."

"Yes, I am, Dad."

"Bullshit! Divorced? Doesn't anyone tell me anything around here?"

"I did tell you, Dad, but you forgot."

"Like hell I forgot."

And so on. Every time she told him, it was like he was hearing the bad news for the first time. After this happened five or six times, we decided that John wasn't going to remember and that it was best to act like nothing had happened. We didn't want to keep upsetting him.

By the time John's food arrives today, he's no longer worrying about how I feel or anything else. He eats like he's going to the electric chair.

John still seems to be doing well, so I see no harm in us driving through Amarillo, especially since, according to my books, it's supposed to have the feel of the old road. We take Business Loop 40, which is old 66, and follow it onto Amarillo Boulevard. Traffic is heavy and while I would usually be nervous about this, I am still abnormally relaxed from the little blue pills. I do see a few old motor lodges—the Apache Motel and such, but the city seems dusty and run-down. When we get around Sixth Street, there is a little area with shops and restaurants. John slows down the van.

"There's some gift shops. Want to stop and take a look?"

I smile at my husband. He is being an absolute dear today.

"No, I think I'm fine, John. Thanks anyway."

He's right, though. There are some cute shops in this area. Ten or fifteen years ago, I would have wanted to stop and look around. Even goofy with discomfort medication, it crosses my mind today. Then I realize that this would be silly.

At one time, that was one of my favorite parts of vacation, the bringing back of things. My personal weakness was pottery. No matter where we traveled, I always came back with a little something—Indian pots from Wyoming and Montana, beautiful glazed vases from Pigeon Forge, Mexican bowls from the South-west. All beautiful, and most of it still packed away in boxes in our basement. A home, after all, only has so much room. I simply had to stop buying things. In later trips, there might have been a trinket or two brought back for the grandchildren, but now we are done with that. I think about all those boxes in the basement. The kids are going to have quite a job ahead of them.

Outside of Amarillo, we pick up I-40 again and I'm feeling a bit more clearheaded. Before long we hit Exit 62 and I direct John off the freeway. I rummage around in one of the storage compartments behind us until I find our old binoculars.

"What are you looking for?" asks John, when he sees what I have in my hands.

"I want to get a look at that Cadillac Ranch," I say, gently unwinding the leather strap that's wound around the glasses, but it's so cracked that it falls apart in my lap. Peeved, I toss the pieces of strap in the litter bag.

"What's that?"

I pick up my guidebook and read. "Says here that it's some sort of art project by an eccentric helium tycoon. It's a bunch of old cars that he buried in the dirt."

John frowns. "Why the hell did he do that?"

I scan the side of the road with the binoculars. "I told you, it's an art project."

"Sounds like a waste of good cars to me." He takes his hat off and adjusts the headband, puts it back on.

"They're old ones from the forties and fifties."

"Oh." He grunts. I can tell John doesn't approve.

I see something far off the road in the middle of a big field, like it says in my book. Way too far for either of us to walk.

"Slow down, John. Would you? I want to take a look."

"I don't see why—"

"Jesus, John! Would you pull over? I just want a look."

"All right, don't get your tit in a wringer."

I swear, sometimes I like him better when he's in one of his fogs. We pull over by a Dumpster covered with graffiti.

"Is that it?"

Through the binoculars, I see a line of cars buried headfirst into the dirt. There are no people around, just a couple of cows grazing nearby. "I think so."

"Doesn't look like they're in good shape," says John.

I hand him the glasses so he can take a look. "No, they aren't. They've been all spray-painted and bashed up. They don't even have tires."

"That's a shame. Why are they buried again?"

"It's an art project, John," I say, after he gives me back the binoculars. Then after a moment, "I have no idea."

Yet the sight of these cars buried in the dirt does something to me. Tailfins pointed up toward the sky, there is something sad and disturbing about them. Our friends and relatives once desired cars like these. They were considered the height of style. We had a neighbor on our old block that lorded his new Cadillacs over us, thought he was better than us because he had a big shiny whale parked in his driveway.

"John, you remember Ed Werner and his Cadillac?"

"Oh yeah."

"That old soak, getting home from work every night, stepping out of his Caddy with his bottle of Cutty Sark."

"Crown Prince Sonny Boy, the car salesman."

John remembers him all right. Now he's long dead and these fancy cars are just junk, like what's here at the Cadillac Ranch.

There was a time in his life when I know John would have liked to own a Cadillac. Not that we could have ever afforded one, not that I would have let him buy one even if we could. Those big cars are just too flashy.

Looking through the binoculars, my vision starts to falter, sweat collects beneath my eyebrows around the lenses. I feel languid and irritated, maybe from my meds, maybe not. This so-called art feels to me like a slap in my generation's face, everything we worked for, everything we thought we needed after the war, our illusions of prosperity. After growing up poor, being middle class seemed like the most wonderful thing anyone could ever hope for.

The Cadillac Ranch gives me a pain in the ass. Oh, excuse me. A *discomfort* in the ass.

At Adrian, Texas, we stop at a little place called the Midpoint Café, located at the exact "Geo-Mathematical" midpoint of Route 66, whatever that means. I finally got my appetite back, even though I'm not sure what I can keep down. They do have homemade "Ugly Crust" pies, which intrigue me.

Our waitress, I'm happy to say, is not at all talkative. She looks as aged as us, which is rare for a waitress. Yet there's no good-natured *"Hello dearie, ain't we old?"* crapola. On her smock, she wears dozens of grandchild (and probably great-grandchild) photo buttons and flag pins. She jangles as she totters about with her slight limp and big sneakers squeaking against the linoleum.

I order banana cream pie for me, apple for John. And milk for both of us. When it comes, I take a big sip and the coldness almost makes me sick at first, then it settles and I know I'll be okay. There's not much to say at the table. John's getting tired and quiet. I'm thinking we should call it a day soon.

The pie is absolutely wonderful. Sweet, but not too sweet, with a lard crust that comes off your fork like little flakes of heaven. After we each finish our slices, we order a slice of co-conut cream and polish that off in no time flat. I feel a lot better with something sweet under my belt.

The waitress leaves our bill on the table without a word. I turn to John, hold up my glass with the last of my milk in it. "We made it halfway, old man."

John holds up his glass and touches it to mine.

How do you find a ghost town? Just look for nothing and there it is.

Actually, you need to get off at Exit 0 (I'm not kidding) and cross to the south side of the freeway where the road is in lousy shape, pockmarked and scattered with gravel. I direct John to turn right toward the old buildings up ahead. We have now entered Glenrio, a real ghost town along the old highway.

"Slow down," I say. We pass an abandoned hotel with a sign in front of it:

LAS   IN TEXAS

Half the sign's busted away, but from my books I know that it used to say LAST HOTEL IN TEXAS on one side and FIRST HOTEL IN TEXAS on the other, depending on which way you were coming. Glenrio is situated in both Texas and New Mexico. The Texas side was located in "Deaf Smith County," the dry part of town. All the bars were on the New Mexico side. The gas stations were on the Texas side, where taxes were less.

We go by the shell of an old gas station. In front of a skeletal gas pump sits a dusty white Pontiac from the '70s, windows busted out, a home to the birds.

"They filmed that movie *The Grapes of Wrath* here, John. Remember? With Henry Fonda? Hard to picture him poking around in this mess."

"I don't like it here," says John.

He's right. There's something unsettling about this place, hollowed out, yet gorged with memories. Still, at least there are ruins here to hint at the past. But they won't be here forever. Slowly, history crumbles away, piece by piece, until even the ghost towns disappear.

I pat a tissue to my forehead. My mouth is so dry, it feels

like I've been snacking on mucilage. "You're going to have to turn around. The road isn't paved up ahead. Just pull off and circle back."

John turns the van around, hits the gas. Just then, there's a sound like a gunshot, which scares the daylights out of me. I hear *chunk-a-chunk,* and the van veers hard to the right, shifting us both in our seats. My armrest jams my side and I just about pass out. The noise gets louder. I yell to John, "What's happening?"

John's too busy holding on to the steering wheel, trying to keep control of the van. I see a vein sticking out on the side of his forehead. I hope he doesn't bust a gusset. The van keeps veering hard as John pumps the brakes. He directs us toward the shoulder.

"Oh shit," he says, his hands white and blue around the steering wheel. "I got it, I got it."

I feel the gravel shift beneath us, the sound of rock crushed into itself, of Post Grape-Nuts amplified by a hundred. I'm sure John is going to lose control. I try to take a breath, but I can only suck air into my lungs, not breathe it out again.

"Ella, stop making that noise," says John. "We've just got a flat tire."

I hear dishes and boxes in the back of the van shift and hit the floor. The crunching noise stops, and the van heaves to a halt on the shoulder, not far from The Last Hotel in Texas. John turns off the engine and we sit there lopsided, listening to ourselves breathe.

Two long minutes pass. John just stares out at the road.

The look on his face is content, like he doesn't have a worry in the world. I'm not scared anymore, but I am getting annoyed. "John," I finally say. "Are you all right?"

He nods.

"Well, what are you waiting for?" I say. "You said we've got a flat tire. Aren't you going to go out there and take a look?"

John turns and stares, as if to say "Who me?"

Finally, he opens his door and climbs out. I decide to join him, so I look behind the seat for my cane, but it's slid back from where I stowed it.

"John!" I yell.

Nothing. I yell his name again. No answer. God only knows what he's doing. I decide to get the damn cane myself. I get so tired of being helpless. I search around behind the seat and find a long telescoping stick with a two-prong fork that grips things. John sometimes uses it to flip open the door lock on my side of the van.

My cane has slid quite a ways back, into the middle of our kitchen area. I hear John making noise, getting something out of a storage area, which only makes me work faster. I lengthen the stick, grab one of the legs of my cane, and drag it toward me, past a loose Corelle plate on the floor.

Outside, I find John with all the equipment out, ready to fix the flat tire. The problem is, I don't think he remembers how to do it. I wish I'd kept my big fat mouth shut. "Let's call the Auto Club," I say.

"I can do it."

I try to be gentle with him. "I know you can, I just don't want you to hurt yourself, honey." I also don't want to be here for hours.

John tries to put the jack together. It's sad to watch. I head back into the van to use the cellular phone. The Auto Club tells me that a tow truck will be here in about forty minutes. I let myself down from the passenger's seat gently, the old discomfort rearing its thorny head again. I find that John has managed to put the jack together, has it under the van, and is cranking away at it, but nothing is happening. The jack is clicking as if it should be raising the van, but something isn't engaged.

"John, the Auto Club's going to fix it. Come on, let's get out of this sun. You shouldn't be out here. You're going to get the skin cancer back on your head."

"Aw, malarkey."

"Come on."

Amazingly, John drops the handle and as we head back to sit in the van, a car blasts past us, the first one we've seen since we got off the highway. I see its brake lights flash. It's an old Plymouth with wide patches of gray primer on the side and trunk. I watch it pull onto the shoulder about a half block up. After a minute, the driver gets out, then the passenger, who is holding a tire iron.

I have to say, they don't look like your typical good Samaritans. They look like sharpies, actually. Both are in their late thirties. The driver has a moustache, tight jeans with a maroon Ban-Lon sport shirt, and a big high pelt of hair. The one holding the lug wrench is just wearing jeans and a V-neck T-shirt and shower thongs. He's got a scrubby beard and hair that looks like he just got up.

"Hey, folks!" the driver yells out as they walk toward us. "Need a hand?"

John looks suspiciously at them.

"We're fine, thank you," I say, smiling. "We just called the Auto Club."

"Oh. Okay. When are they expected?" says the passenger.

"Probably a half hour or so." Just then, something tells me I've said the wrong thing.

"That's fine," says the driver, pulling a knife from the back of his belt.

"Oh dear," I say. I look over at John, who hasn't realized what's going on yet.

"We don't need any help," says John, pulling off his cap, wiping the sweat from his head with his wrist, then snugging the hat back down again.

"We're not here to help," says the passenger with the lug wrench. Maybe it's his accent, but he doesn't sound too bright.

John starts to understand. "What the hell," he says, stepping forward.

"John, take it easy."

The driver points at John with his knife. "Sir, you stay where you are. We're going to need all your cash and then we'll leave. We don't want to hurt either of you two, but I don't think it would be too difficult. Ma'am, I see you have a ring, why don't you take it off?"

The passenger, wielding the tire iron, walks up to John. "Wallet."

"Fuck you," says John.

The passenger pokes John in the ribs with the tire iron. "I'll just get it myself then," he says, reaching toward John's bulging back pocket.

"John, do what they say," I say, handing my wedding ring to the driver. "You stay put."

"I'll need your purse, ma'am. Where is it?"

"It's on the floor of the van," I say.

"Damn," says the passenger, fiddling with the back of John's pants. "I can't get his wallet out of his pants pocket. It's enormous. Bring that knife here."

"It's a big wallet," I say. "I'll get my purse."

He looks at me, narrowing his eyes. "Do it very slowly, ma'am."

"That's the only way I do anything, young man." I press my cane into the gravel to walk myself to the open door of the van.

I hear them cursing away at John's pants, then the tearing of fabric. I don't know if it's fatigue or the narcotics coursing through my veins or the fact that it made me very, very mad to give these cretins my wedding ring, but I know what I need to do. I don't really give it a moment's consideration.

When I turn back around from the van, I see that they have cut a plaid trapdoor in the back of John's pants. The driver and passenger are laughing at their handiwork, until they look up at me, pointing John's gun at them.

"Oh shit," says the passenger, dropping his tire iron. The driver starts to raise his knife.

"Please don't do that," I say to him. "It's a bad idea."

The driver looks surprised to have an old woman train a gun on his heart. He holds the knife down by his thigh, tightening his grip on it. "He's right here, ma'am. I could hurt him. You better put that down."

"Yes you could, but I will definitely kill you. And if you think I'm afraid to do that, young man, you're terribly wrong. You should understand that there is absolutely nothing for me to lose. I suppose you feel that way, otherwise you wouldn't do awful things like this, but for me, it's true. If you hurt John, I will most certainly kill you and do my best to kill your friend. I am long past the point of caring."

The driver looks at the passenger, trying to figure out what he can get away with.

"It's not going to work," I say, taking careful aim, ready to shoot if he moves toward John. "Put down that knife."

"Don't forget to turn off the safety before you shoot him," says John.

"Thank you, dear," I say. "But it's already off."

"Let's go, Steve," says the passenger, his voice quaking. "Give them their shit back."

I nod. "He's right, Steve. Put the ring on the wallet and just put it on the ground and then you can get out of here. I'm not even going to call the police. I just want you to go away."

Finally, Steve drops the knife and does what I say. He stands up, waiting to see what I do next.

"Now go," I say, flicking my hand at him. "Find something to do with your life and stop bothering old people. You should be ashamed of yourself. You're going to wind up a fish fly in your next life."

They run back to their car. The passenger runs so fast, he leaves one of his flip-flops along the side of the road. They tear ass out of there.

No sooner do I toss the knife into the brush and put my wedding ring back on, than the Auto Club arrives. Early. Wouldn't you know it?

The tow truck operator is a stern young Mexican man with a shaved head. His mechanic's shirt has the sleeves ripped off. No name patch but he does have a large tattoo of Our Lady of Guadalupe from his shoulder to his elbow. I've seen her on a lot of calendars and such out this way. The young man doesn't say much, just nods at us, asks for our AAA card, fills out a slip on a clipboard, and asks John to sign.

"I'll sign it," I say.

John frowns at me, then signs the slip. He nods at the mechanic. "Beautiful day, isn't it, young man?" Apparently, an attempt on his life puts John in a jovial mood.

"Yes sir," says the mechanic dully, just barely meeting John's gaze.

"I like your haircut." John then lifts his golf cap to reveal his empty scalp. "I've got the same one."

The mechanic tips his head, trying hard to maintain his

stone face, trying not to smile at John's comment. Then he just shakes his head and starts to laugh.

John used to always have this effect on people. Maybe his hokey patter reminds people of their father, I don't know, but it's amazing who he wins over.

Smiling now, the young man looks over at me. I'm sure I look a fright.

"Are you all right, ma'am? You want to sit in my truck while I change the tire? I can turn on the air-conditioning."

Sometimes the world is a much easier place to figure out when people act badly. You know what to do then. A small act of kindness is another thing altogether.

"I . . . That would be nice," I stammer, all of it suddenly catching up with me.

He slips his clipboard under his arm and opens the door to his truck. "Yeah, come on. The sun is strong out here."

Once I'm in the clammy tow truck with the air-conditioning blasting, the waterworks start. The tears come and come and I don't seem to be able to stop myself. I want to say that it's just from being so scared of those two maniacs, but I actually wasn't that scared. I felt like things were going to work out and we would be all right. Tell you one thing, I sure as hell wasn't going to let them get away with my ring. And for the record, I most certainly would have shot them both. (Though I haven't fired a gun in twenty years, and then it was just a few afternoons at the range with John. But I was good at it.) I guess it could be any number of things—the holdup, the flat tire, the seemingly endless discomfort I'm experiencing, or maybe just that this trip will be over soon and I don't know what will become of us. Or maybe I do know and I'm afraid to think about that. I guess it's all of it.

John turns to me and says very seriously, "Are you all right, miss?"

All this excitement has had its effect on him, too. I'm just glad he's forgotten about his gun. "I'm all right, John." I pull a tissue from my sleeve, blow my nose in it. I don't know what else to do with it, so I just put it back in my sleeve.

Within minutes, the young man has replaced the tire and we're ready to go. He helps us out of the tow truck and hands us a business card with a big greasy thumbprint on it.

"You guys should probably have this patched before you go any farther. Our place is just up the road in Tucumcari. We'll give you a twenty percent AAA discount."

We thank the young man for all his help. Once situated in the Leisure Seeker, we head back out onto I-40. As he drives, I notice that John holds the tow truck driver's card between his thumb and the steering wheel, as if he doesn't want to forget. At the exit for Tucumcari, John turns to me and says, "I think we ought to get that tire fixed right away."

"If you think so," I say, happy to have him acting like a man for a change.

As we enter the city of Tucumcari, I feel the sweats come on. It feels just like menopause again. Believe me, once was bad enough. Luckily, the gas station that we're looking for is right on Route 66 in town, not far past a cute little place called the Blue Swallow Motel.

After we pull into the lot, the young Mexican man comes up to the window. Despite the encroaching discomfort, I smile at him, but he doesn't say hi, he doesn't say anything. He just stands there. I wait for John to speak. After all, he's still holding the business card, but he clams up, too.

"We're taking you up on your offer," I say, leaning over John. "How much will it be to fix the tire?"

The young man looks bewildered for a moment, then says, "You have the blowout at Glenrio?"

I nod yes. "Yes, and you—"

"That was my brother," he says, cutting me off. "He changed your tire."

"Oh," I say, a bit embarrassed. "I'm sorry." I look at his forearm. No tattoo. Same haircut, though.

"Fourteen dollars. Be a half hour." Without even waiting for me to agree, he heads toward the back of the van where he pulls the flat off the mount, then heads for the garage.

After John parks the van in the shade, I hand him a box of Sociables and discreetly take the keys from the ignition. I'm going to take a nap and I don't want to wake up in Timbuktu. I take a little blue pill. The last thing I remember before I doze off is John settling in with the crackers and a Louis L'Amour paperback that I've seen him read at least a dozen times. It must feel new to him each time he picks it up. I guess we save a lot of money on books that way.

Eight

NEW MEXICO

We keep gaining time. Yet even with an extra hour from the time change, the few miles to the KOA Kampground just outside Tucumcari seems to take forever. I'm feeling better, no longer shaking, but John hasn't said an intelligible word since we got here. He's yawning and talking to himself, his window of lucidity squandered by nincompoops.

Once we set up, John sits down at the table inside the van. I put a can of Pepsi and a bowl of chips in front of him, and he promptly falls asleep.

Happy for the time alone, I mix myself a highball of Vernors and Canadian Club in a green aluminum camp cup and head outside to the picnic table. I bring my cane and sit down carefully, with my back to the table so I can get up easily. I take that first sip and smile. In the distance, I hear these sounds: the scream of a child that alarms me at first, but then when it's followed by the voice of a different child, I realize they are only playing; the nasal putter of a small airplane flying above the campground; the distant *bah-dumm* of a car passing over a seam in the road out on I-40.

The Vernors, even mixed with whiskey, is still so spicy and sharply carbonated that it makes me cough a bit. (As a young woman, I drank Boston Coolers at the Vernors factory down at the foot of Woodward Avenue, not far from the river. A scoop of Sanders vanilla floating in shimmery gingery pop—the first sip could actually make you sneeze.) I'm glad we brought a twelve-pack of Vernors from Detroit. You can't always get it in other parts of the country. It's a local specialty, you know.

It may be my imagination, but I already feel the effects of the C.C. A radiance spreads through my chest, a tingle, and I remember the second dose of anti-discomfort medicine I took today. I guess I'm turning into quite the—what's the expression Oprah likes to use?—*substance abuser.*

I take another sip of my highball.

The campground, while not deserted, isn't exactly crowded. A young couple approaches, pushing a stroller. I wave to them, but they ignore me. Neither parent looks over eighteen years of age. What they are doing camping with a baby, I don't know.

"Hi!" I call out to them. "How old is your little one?"

At first I think they're going to keep walking, but then the girl looks back at me, then over to the boy. He lowers his head into his shoulders like a tortoise. Finally, she turns to me and yells back.

"She's seven months old, ma'am."

"She's darling," I say, though I can't really tell. Something about their shyness makes me bolder. Besides, I want to see a baby. After this day, I need to see a baby.

I speak up. "Come on over. Let me have a closer look. Come on, I won't bite."

They both shuffle toward me, heads down. A scrawnier set of parents I have never seen. They barely look weaned themselves.

"That's better," I say, once they're in front of me. Up close, I see how young they are, sixteen or seventeen, tops. She's gaunt and pale, with dun-colored hair and light hazel eyes, a leaf of a girl. Her beige top is cut short, exposing her tiny waist. Even there with a baby, she seems gawky, unaccustomed to her woman's body. The boy's face is tight and oblong, with a high forehead and thin brown hair that doesn't have a bright future ahead of it. His T-shirt says OLD NAVY ATHLETIC DEPARTMENT, but that's the only thing that's athletic about him.

I see how worn their clothes are, how tired they look. Even the baby just lies there, violet lids half closed, tiny fingers raised and stirring like sea grass.

"Oh, she's adorable," I lie. "What's her name?"

"Britney," says the girl, making it sound like a question. That upward lilt in her voice reminds me of our granddaughter, Lydia.

"That's a pretty name. What's yours?"

"I'm Tiffany. That's Jesse."

The boy squints at me with the same dark eyes as the child. "Well, I'm Ella. It's so nice to meet you. You've got a beautiful baby."

"Really?" When Tiffany smiles, she looks about fourteen.

"Of course she is," I say, wondering what people have been telling her. "Where are you two headed?"

"Ohio? His aunt and uncle are there."

"Oh. Are you visiting?" I'm shameless, but I need to know.

"We're gonna live there," she says, eyes shifting downward. He squeezes her elbow, and she moves closer to him.

"Well, that sounds nice. You'll like it around there. We're from Michigan. Right here." I hold my right hand up, palm forward, and point to just below the lowest knuckle of my thumb to show them where Detroit is. Suddenly, they both break into uncontrollable giggles.

It takes me a moment to catch on. "Oh. That's what we do in Michigan when we want to show where a town is located."

"Really?" says Tiffany, still laughing.

I nod. "Because it's shaped like a hand."

"It is?" she says, half smiling.

"Uh-huh. Do you two have a camper?"

"No. We got a tent," she says, obviously not pleased about the situation.

"That must be hard with a baby," I say.

Tiffany nods vigorously. Finally, the boy speaks: "We should go."

"You just got here," I say. "Would you like something to eat?" Jesse's eyes widen ever so slightly, and I realize that I've asked the magic question. "How about a sandwich? I'm sure I've got something for the baby, too."

They look at each other again, each waiting for the other to answer.

"Then it's settled," I say. "You sit down right here at the table and I'll have some dinner ready in a jiffy."

It doesn't take much prodding to get them to sit down. Then I pop into the camper and give John a poke. "John, we've got company," I say, snatching the bowl of chips off the table.

"Who's here?" he says, sounding grumpy as hell.

I don't know what to say, so I improvise. "It's the kids. And they brought the baby!"

John gets up, walks out of the van, all smiles. "Hey there, you two!" he says to Tiffany and Jesse, who look befuddled, but grin anyway, caught up in the warmth of John's bonhomie.

When he sees the baby, that's all she wrote. "And who's this little girl? Look at her. What a sweetie pie. *Yes, she is.*" Peekaboo is played. Noses are stolen and returned repeatedly. Some color comes to Tiffany's and Jesse's cheeks as they watch.

Sometimes we need a little social pressure to be at our best.

I make grilled ham and cheese sandwiches in the electric frying pan and heat up a couple of cans of chicken noodle soup. We crack a tub of potato salad from the fridge. I find an applesauce cup and cut up a ripe banana for the baby. An hour later, the kids are full, and little Britney smiles every time she lays eyes on John.

Tiffany and Jesse have never heard any of John's stories before and tonight they're happy to listen. I'm happy to take care of them all. Tonight, we all make believe that we are other people. We don't talk about their problems or our problems. The kids hardly even talk. Though Tiffany happens to mention that back home in Tempe, Britney would always wake up and start crying in the middle of the night.

"Do you ever take her for a drive?" I say.

Tiffany scrunches her chalky face at me like I'm off my rocker. "Noooo."

"That helps."

"Really?"

I make an effort not to frown. "You've never heard that? It's the movement that soothes them. You try it and see if it doesn't help. It always worked on my kids, and I know my Cynthia used it on her little boy when he wouldn't stop crying. That or she ran the vacuum cleaner."

Tiffany's pointy brows squeeze together. The crazy look again. "Whaaat?"

Despite all this lip I'm getting, it pleases me to give this poor girl a little grandmotherly advice. I don't think she's been getting a whole lot of it.

Then I wonder to myself: Does a feeling of movement soothe a new baby in the same way it soothes an old woman? It doesn't seem like it should, but somehow this makes sense to me. New to the earth and not long for it somehow don't seem so different these days.

Before they leave, I give the kids extra blankets. In the van, I make up a bag filled with canned goods, cookies, and things for their cooler. From my cupboard, I grab an old Tupperware container. I take off the lid, put in a wad of tens and twenties from my hiding place, burp the air out, seal it tight, and place it at the bottom of the bag.

The next morning we both have a hard time getting out of bed. After two very strong cups of instant Folgers each, we pack up and hit I-40. (No patience at the moment for flitting between freeway and old road.) For a long time, neither John nor I say anything. This is rare, for as you know, I'm usually prattling away, giving directions, asking John if he remembers things, trying to fill the air with words as if I can't bear the silence, which isn't far from the truth. But right now, the only sounds are the leaden howl of the Leisure Seeker's V-8 and the *frapp-frapp* of untucked maps between our seats being whipped by the wind.

I don't speak because I can't stop looking at the sky, at its long yawning unending face. It is the biggest, brightest, bluest sky I've ever seen. It hurts to look at it, but I can't stop. I scan its cloudless expanse, my eyes flicking here and there and here, shifting every which way, like those pictures I've seen on TV of the way our eyes move as we dream. My heart fluttering and catching, I search this aching span, waiting for it to tear itself open and reveal what I know is there: a roaring vacuum that sucks everything into it that's not nailed down.

I think maybe someone had a little too much coffee this morning.

When I realize this, my eyes finally pause and rest in one place. That's when I can't help but be stunned, plain old whopperjawed, by the beauty of this sky. As for its size, well, the sheer immensity of it makes me feel so insignificant that I realize that all my problems will ultimately pass with nary a soul noticing. It's then that I find calm.

I look over at John and see the coffee has got him juiced up and crazy as well. He has his flag hat pulled down low over his eyes, making his ears stick out like Dumbo. He's loaded for bear, determined to get some miles under our belt. These long-ago ways of ours die hard. It's good that we're on the freeway. Anyway, it won't be long before I-40 meets up with a good-sized stretch of 66 past Clines Corners.

I touch my finger to my upper lip and it feels damp. The discomfort is back, but it's a new brutal-edged kind, a searing hot blade tempered on the entrails. The kind of discomfort that makes me want to talk to my children. I drop the guidebook that I'm holding, open the glove box, and start fumbling around for the cellular phone.

"John? Did you do something with the phone?"

Blandly, John looks at me. "I didn't touch it."

This happens all the time at home. John hides things. He can no longer be trusted to put things away where they belong.

"Yes, you did. I left it in here in the glove box after I called the Auto Club. Where did you put it?"

He scowls at me. "I didn't touch your goddamn phone."

He's getting mad, but I don't care. I'm so goddamned tired of his bullshit. I pull everything from the glove box. No phone. I'm just about to start crying.

"Goddamn it, John!" I scream. "I know you did something with it. What did you *do* with it?"

"Shove it up your ass!" bellows John.

"You shove it up your ass, you senile old bastard. *Where did you put it?*"

Then I remember that on the shelf near the dash, by the cup holders, there's a rectangular slot, a catchall compartment. I can't see inside it, but I can reach down in there. I feel something that could be an antenna.

Bingo. It's the cell phone.

"Why the hell did you hide it in there, John?"

"I told you, I didn't put it there."

That's when I remember that *I* put it in there after the last time I used it. In fact, I put it in there specifically so John wouldn't hide it somewhere.

"Idiot," I mutter.

"Drop dead," says John.

"Oh, stop being such a pistol. I'm talking about myself."

I roll up the window and turn the phone on. It makes a series of musical tones that are there to distract you from the fact that you're about to shoot microwaves into your brain. I think about taking a little blue pill, but I push the idea from my mind and instead punch in Cindy's cell phone number, not sure if she's got it turned on at work. But she answers immediately.

"Hi honey," I say, so happy to hear my daughter's voice that I can almost feel the pain recede.

"Mom?"

"Of course it's your mother. Who did you think?"

"Mom. Where are you?" I ignore the exasperation in her voice. I hope I'm not getting her in trouble.

"Can you talk?"

"I'm on my break, Mom. Where *are* you?"

"We're somewhere in New Mexico. It's beautiful here. Honey, you should see the sky—"

Cindy cuts me off. "We've all been worried sick about you two. Thank God you're all right. You have to come home, Mom."

The last thing on earth I want to do is get in an argument with my daughter today. I'm just so happy to hear her voice. "Cynthia, there's nothing to worry about. We're both feeling great. Really, it's been so much fun."

She exhales loudly, as if she doesn't believe me. I suppose I am laying it on a bit thick, but I'm trying to reassure her and maybe myself, too.

"You've got to come home." Her voice is coarse, thick with emotion and cigarettes. I do wish she'd quit.

"Cindy, sweetie."

"It's just that you're so sick. I'm just afraid—"

I don't let her finish. I don't need to hear her say this any more than she needs to say it. "Dear, what's going to happen is going to happen. It's all right. We all have to be all right with it, okay?"

"Damn it, Mom." She's cursing, but her voice is whispery now, deflated. "Kevin keeps wanting to call the police."

"Well, you tell Kevin that that's a bad idea. He's just going to make things worse. He's going to turn us into Bonnie and Clyde."

It occurs to me that we've already pulled a gun on some people and threatened to kill them. It's too late. We *are* Bonnie and Clyde.

She clears her throat. "How's Dad?"

"Your father is fine. He's full of beans. He still has his little spells, but he's doing all right. His driving has been very good. You want to talk to him?"

Snuffle. "Okay."

I'm a little worried about him driving and talking on a phone at the same time, but I need a break to compose myself. I hand the phone over to John. "Roll up your window for a minute so you can talk on the phone."

"Who is this?" John says, as he cranks the window up.

"It's your daughter, dummy," I say. "It's Cynthia." I say her name so he remembers to say it to her.

"Hi, Chuckles," John says. Where did he pull out that from? He hasn't called her Chuckles since the third grade. It was her favorite candy.

John is smiling like all get-out, so pleased to talk to his

163

daughter. I don't know if he thinks he's talking to a little girl or what, but what does it matter if he's happy and Cindy feels better?

"We'll be careful, kiddo," John says. "Love you. We'll see you soon." He hands me the phone.

"Cindy?" I say.

"Yeah, Mom?" Her voice is brighter now. She sounds better, which makes me feel better.

"I love you, too." The pain is coming back, but I don't really care at the moment.

"Me, too." Cindy lets out a ragged little wheeze. "Please be careful. Come home soon."

I nod, then catch myself. "Give our love to Lydia and Joey. Tell your brother we called."

"I will." She breathes loudly into the phone and I can hear her voice break. "Bye, Mommy."

I push the off button. My eyes are burning and I'm not sure if it's the exhaust fumes filtering into the van, or the fact that my fifty-seven-year-old daughter, the one who has always been the tough, defiant child, the one who has sassed me since she was eight, just called me Mommy.

We are traveling through the foothills of the Rockies, surrounded by mountains. Suddenly, I need to talk now, I need to know that I am still here, still able to make a noise. I point at the mountains far to the north of us.

"See those mountains, John?"

"What?"

"Those mountains over in the distance." John says nothing. He just yawns. Apparently I'm still here. I'm just boring.

"Those are the *Sangre de Cristo* Mountains," I say.

John looks at me. "Crisco?" he says. "Like the shortening?"

"*Cristo*. It means Blood of Christ," I say.

"Hmph," says John, sneering. "Christ, my ass."

So ends our talk. In case you haven't guessed, John is not a religious man. I suppose you could call him an atheist. His parents never instilled in him any sense of religion or God, and that's probably where it started, but it was going off to war in his teens that made him a full-fledged heathen. He used to say that watching the head of the person standing next to you disappear doesn't make you much feel like there's a god.

When he came home from the war, John *was* different. He was no longer the boy from the neighborhood who pestered me like a gnat, asking me out all the time. I must have turned him down a dozen times. He was always saying that he was going to marry me. I'd laugh in his face, not in a mean way, but it was still laughing. He was younger than the boys I was dating, and I wasn't attracted.

Eventually, I became engaged to another boy, but something happened to him during the war. You're probably thinking I'm going to say he was killed, but you'd be wrong. The SOB dumped me. Yes, threw me over *during* the war. I was the only person I know that this happened to. I knew girls getting married, engaged, pregnant, you name it. I knew girls whose boyfriends, fiancés, husbands were killed or missing in action, but I was the only one I knew who got the old heave-ho by their GI Joe. Charlie met someone else while stationed in Texas, some round-heeled Armenian broad. He wound up marrying her, after knocking her up.

But John made it back. I guess the most attractive thing about him then, aside from the fact that he had gotten bigger and quieter, was that he seemed no longer interested in me. He had written often during the first year he was away, telling me how much he looked forward to seeing me again, how much he missed home. (Decades later, he showed me photographs he had taken during the war, and I remember being struck by how young everyone was. They looked like high school boys, posing with no shirts on, holding heavy-looking guns, displaying Japanese flags that they had recovered from the bodies of soldiers that they had killed. All those boys, acting brave and cocky. I remember John pointing out in the photos who died and who had made it back.)

As for his letters, I only answered once or twice. It wasn't personal, I just wasn't much of a letter writer. I was always kind of self-conscious about my writing skills. And I was still engaged to Charlie, anyway. As these things tend to happen, John stopped writing right around the same time Charlie dropped me.

When the war ended and I heard that John was home, I expected to hear from him. I could've used an ego boost, a little cheering up, but he never came by. It had been a bad time for my family. We lost my brother Tim at the Battle of the Bulge. We didn't know how it happened or anything else, just that he was dead. That's how they did things then. A goddamned telegram.

Then a month or so after V-J Day, John just appeared at the doorstep of my family's house. He had seen the gold star up on our door and knew it was for Timmy. He wanted to stop by to pay his respects to my mother. We got to talking and I could tell he was still interested in me, though he was fighting it off.

Later he told me that he had promised himself that he wasn't going to come see me, but when he saw the star, he knew he had to. We sat there in the front room of the old house and talked about Timmy, whom he had barely known.

When I asked John about what happened to him, he told me that he had been wounded on the island of Leyte in the Pacific, how the bullet entered the back of his ankle, how it wasn't that bad, but it was enough to send him home because it would take so long to heal. He told me how while he was in the hospital, all the guys in his unit had gone down in a plane crash over the Pacific. When I told him how lucky he was, he called it his "million-dollar bullet hole."

There was a quiet moment, then he said, "Why didn't you write to me?"

"I was engaged to Charlie," I said, afraid he would ask me that. "It didn't seem right."

"How is Charlie?"

I remember lowering my eyes to the faded floral print of the parlor rug, then finally up at him. "He's living in Texas with his new wife."

John looked at me and grinned. "Yeah, I know."

That little shit knew all along that Charlie had dropped me. Anyway, we started seeing each other and that time it took.

I lean over and put my hand on John's knee. He turns and looks at me. He smiles, but his eyes tell me that he is not all there at the moment.

Clines Corners is yet another tourist trap. We pull into the big trading post and I decide to look around a little. We could stand to pick up a few provisions and this place is as good as any.

Inside, there's a restaurant along with the store, about the fortieth Route 66 Diner we've seen so far, all with the same old stuff—gas station signs, gas pumps, pictures of James Dean and Elvis and Marilyn Monroe with pink and neon and chrome and, of course, Route 66 signs. I have to say, this decor is getting a little tiresome. It's like visiting the same place over and over.

I buy some cold Pepsis and a bag of Combos for John, while he fills up the tank. The man at the cash register hands me my change. Through the window behind him, I see John finishing up, getting back into the van. I remember that I didn't take the keys this time. I cram the money in my purse, grab the bag, then hustle on out there fast as my cane can support me, before John takes off.

"John!" I yell to him. He doesn't hear, but when I finally get to the van, he's waiting nice as you please. I, on the other hand, am exhausted and panting.

"You all right?" he says.

I glower at him over my glasses. "Fine," I wheeze.

Back on 66, it's much quieter. The landscape is strange, both green and brown, a shaggy blend of desert and forest, as if it can't quite make up its mind what it wants to be. Nipping at the Pepsi, I start to feel a little better. When I go to put my change into my wallet, I notice someone has written something on one of the singles, on the border just above George Washington's head:

god please get me a woman

I flip over the other side and it says:

give me relief

"Look at this," I say to John.

John takes the bill, reads both sides, and frowns. "He's barking up the wrong tree."

"Smartass," I say. Maybe he's in better shape than I think today.

━━━━

We drive the old route toward Albuquerque, which has become Scenic Road 333 instead of Route 66. It is a gnarled, narrow road that lowers us into Tijeras Canyon, pulls us out, and then lowers us again. The walls of the canyon rise from the road, ridged and crenellated, covered with a burnt layer of brush. Everything looks weathered, shriveled, half-dead. It reminds me that we're only a couple hundred miles from Alamogordo, where they tested the first A-bomb. It looks like it.

I know only too well about the effects of radiation, the barrenness it causes, all the good it's supposed to do while it destroys. I have watched too many friends and relations wither and die, not from their disease, but from this alleged cure for their disease. That's why I told Dr. Tom and all the rest of them that there no way they were going to use that stuff on me. The kids were all gung ho about aggressive treatment, but I told them: no radiation, no chemo, no nothing. The doctors seemed actually relieved. They don't like using most of that stuff on old people, anyway. Of course, they don't want you to go out and enjoy yourself, either. They just want you to rot in some hospital somewhere, while they do their tests on you and do everything humanly possible to keep you alive and uncomfortable for as long as possible; then when they feel like they've done everything they can, they send you home to die. I suppose they think that's the best place to die. It probably is, for most people.

I decide we need some distraction. "John, let's drive around Albuquerque a little bit, see what's here. What do you say?"

"All right with me."

We follow the business loop into the old section of town, where we have a gander at the Pueblo architecture, the old KiMo and El Rey movie theaters, and some crazy murals that look like they were painted by someone with a large supply of discomfort medication. Oh, and you better believe that there's another Route 66 Diner. Gee, maybe there's posters of Marilyn Monroe and James Dean in there.

We climb Nine Mile Hill and in my rearview mirror, I watch Albuquerque diminish. We take the Old Town Bridge over the Rio Grande. The water below is dark and filthy. Down the road, I see a loose-planked white house with a Polack blue roof. On the side of the house, in block letters, it says:

L-A TRUCKERS CHURCH
ALLELUJA HE IS RISEN
SMOKE FREE BINGO
TUES 6:30

Good to know, I think.

We find a decent campground near a town called Grants. I'm happy to be settled in for the night, happy that our part of the campground is deserted. I've had enough of humanity to last me for a while.

John is suddenly perky, so he sets up the canopy and even drags a picnic table over for me to cook on. Once he turns the place into a proper campsite, I start to relax. It's a lovely afternoon, the air cooling down nicely.

Afterward, John plops down into one of our old aluminum lawn chairs with the frayed green-and-white webbing. (We bought them at the same time we got the Leisure Seeker thirty years ago, so I keep wondering when he's going to bust right through one of them.) He's reading that Louis L'Amour book again, though I haven't seen him turn a page yet. Wouldn't surprise me to see him holding it upside down sometime.

I set up the electric pan out on the picnic table and start frying bologna. I'm not really in the mood for it and I guarantee you that I shouldn't be eating it, but I went through our little fridge and noticed that it was starting to turn. I'd hate for it to go bad, so it's going to be dinner.

I split the edges of the slices so they don't curl much, but once I put them on the frying pan, I don't pay as much attention as I should and the pieces blacken on one side before I remember to flip them. I flop them onto some paper towel to drain the grease. Then I put them between slices of stale Wonder bread, slather on mustard, and serve it with the remains of an old bag of chips and some tepid pickles. All I can say for this meal is that it is quite thoroughly stale. Well done, Ella.

Yet when we sit down at the table, John is thrilled. He gobbles up his sandwich in a matter of minutes, then the other half of mine. I mix myself a manhattan, park myself next to him, take his hand, and we watch the sun set without saying a word.

Once it's dark, the campground gets so damn quiet, I don't know what to do with myself. At the table, John has dozed off next to me. "John, wake up," I say. "You're not going to be able to sleep tonight."

He lifts his head, stares crossly at me. "What?"

"Come on. We're going to watch slides."

"It's too late." He starts to doze again.

I poke him in the shoulder. "Come on. It's just past eight. If we go to bed now, we'll be up at three in the morning. Get out the projector."

"I don't know where it is."

"I'll show you. Put it on the picnic table and then we'll have ice cream."

"All right." He lumbers up from the bench.

Food. It always works.

Tonight the pictures that we project on the side of our trailer are of our children, whom I miss so much, whom I've missed since they started leaving our home decades ago. Although we never exactly intended to do it, we have a tray of slides culled from other trays, a mishmash, entirely of the kids. It allows us to watch our children grow up in the space of about ten minutes, though not necessarily in the correct order. It's like the Greatest Hits of the Robinas.

We see our children swimming at a beach, with birthday

cake smeared on their faces, lying thrilled in piles of fallen leaves, standing stiffly in front of mantels with prom dates, sitting on docks at sunset, staring up at the stone white faces of Mount Rushmore, on the knees of florid Santa Clauses, hugging Mickey Mouse, coming home sunburned and peeling from their very own first vacations without us.

"That's a cute one of Cindy!" John says, shoveling the last spoonful of melted ice cream into his mouth. "She's a little doll." It's a slide of her dressed as a hula girl when she was about twelve. The picture, reddened with age, has made her look older than she really was at the time.

Another shot is of Kevin, barely four, on the same Halloween. He's dressed as a little Indian, with his face painted and a feathered headdress. It's strange to see this here in New Mexico, not far from the Indian reservation.

"Kevin and I got that costume over at Checker's," says John.

I look over at John, amazed. I am constantly mystified by what John ends up remembering. Checker Drugs was a place in our old neighborhood where we went for bread and milk and the occasional vanilla phosphate. I just don't understand why he's able to hang on to information like that, while so many other more important memories evaporate. Then again, I suppose so much of what stays with us is often insignificant. The memories we take to the ends of our lives have no real rhyme or reason, especially when you think of the endless things that you do over the course of a day, a week, a month, a year, a lifetime. All the cups of coffee, hand-washings, changes of clothes, lunches, goings to the bathroom, headaches, naps, walks to school, trips to the grocery store, conversations about the weather—all the things so unimportant that they should be immediately forgotten.

Yet they aren't. I often think of the Chinese red bathrobe I had when I was twenty-seven years old; the sound of our first cat Charlie's feet on the linoleum of our old house; the hot rarefied air around an aluminum pot the moment before all the kernels of popcorn burst open. I think of these things as often as I think about getting married or giving birth or the end of the Second World War. What is truly amazing is that before you know it, sixty years go by and you can remember maybe eight or nine important events, along with a thousand meaningless ones. How can that be?

You want to think there's a pattern to it all because it makes you feel better, gives you some sense of a reason why we're here, but there really isn't any. People look for God in these patterns, these reasons, but only because they don't know where else to look. Things happen to us: some of it important, most of it not, and a little of it stays with us till the end. What stays after that? I'll be damned if I know.

The next slide is Kevin at the Autorama, holding a small trophy and a model car that he had entered in a contest. He won third place. I'm sure he still remembers this day. All I remember is being relieved when we left.

I touch the projector button and the next slide is nothing. There is no next slide, only the very bright light that occurs when the tray slot is empty. I look over at John and he's back in his lawn chair, slumped over asleep. I say his name, but he snorts and goes right back to sleep. He won't be able to move tomorrow. He'll bitch about how sore he is, and then he'll bitch about it again five minutes later.

I hear a noise down the road. It's probably just a little critter, but I start to get scared. Maybe it's a coyote or a wolf. I remember that we are in the campground pretty much by ourselves, that I haven't seen a manager or another person for hours. I decide to get my purse out of the van. I wouldn't mind having that gun nearby. I start to get up, when I hear a noise again—a scrabbling in what is probably a trash can.

"John, wake up!" I yell, determined to head for the van. I grab my cane and try to lift myself up from the picnic table bench, but I've been sitting for too long. My legs are stiff and I can barely feel them. I have to dangle them from the bench to get the blood stirring again. Meanwhile, the fan from the projector is still whirring away, the light blazing. You're not supposed to leave the light on for this long without slides, but I'm not going to turn it off and be left in the dark.

"John!"

"Who is it?" says John, rattled.

"It's *Ella*," I say. "There's a noise up the way." I try my legs and can feel them a little now. I raise myself again, using both hands on the bench of the picnic table. I leave my cane just standing there. I manage to lift myself, but as I reach for my cane, my legs simply fold beneath me. I go down slowly, my knees hit the ground, then my hands, then I topple over onto my side into the hard dirt. I've scraped my hands, my knees are on fire, and my one leg is bent back slightly. I pray it's not broken.

"John!" I yell to him. "I fell!"

"What?"

I'm trying hard not to panic. "I'm on the ground! I *fell,* John! Help me up!"

"Oh, Jesus Christ," John says, as if annoyed. But before I know it, I see the shadow of him above me.

"Take my hand. Take my hand."

"John, you can't lift me up. I weigh too much. You'll fall, too."

"Yes, I can. Just take my hand."

So I take John's hand while he holds on to the picnic table and tries to lift me. He gets me about a foot up from the ground, so I'm able to straighten out my leg before his grip on the table gives out and he comes tumbling forward. *Oh God no,* I think, as his thick, lumbering form towers toward me. I cannot believe this is happening.

"Ahhhhk," yells John. "I—"

I fall back again, but now with John on top of me. This time, it's not a slow, soft fall. It hurts much worse with John's weight on me. Stones bite into my rear end, my head hits the dirt, my insides hurt. I feel the entire mass of his body on me. I can't breathe. I feel more discomfort than I can even describe. Tears push themselves from the corners of my eyes. The first words out of my mouth ache my lungs. "God *damn* it."

John just lies there without doing anything. I can't move with him on top of me. "John, get off me!" I manage to say, almost breathless.

"I think I hurt my arm," he says.

"I don't care. You can't keep lying on top of me. Get off." He stays like a dead weight at first, then I feel his legs start to stir. "John, you're crushing me. Get *off*."

Finally, John sniffs, takes a long, rusty breath, manages to lift himself up and roll over next to me. His arm seems to be all right.

Now at least, I can breathe again. I look over at him. His eyes are crazy and scared. Lord, this is a big mess we're in now, I'm afraid.

My leg feels okay now. It hurts, but I don't think it's broken.

"John. Are you all right?"

He looks at me as if trying to recognize me, then finally he says, "What are you doing down here?"

"John. I fell, remember? You tried to help me up and you fell. We're camping. We're in New Mexico."

"Mexico?"

"*New* Mexico. You fell asleep while we were watching slides. Now we're stuck on the ground."

"Oh, shit," he says.

Even he realizes that we're in trouble. I start to scoot toward the van, still thinking about my purse. Stones dig into my hands as I lift myself from the ground just enough to move inch by inch. I can't believe how filthy I'm getting. My slacks are going to be ruined. But I guess that won't matter if I can't ever get up from the ground.

After a foot or two, I'm not so sure the purse is going to help any. I could shoot the gun until someone shows up, but there's no guarantee that will happen. Besides, I'm afraid to shoot the gun in the air. Back in Detroit, people are always shooting guns into the sky on New Year's Eve and someone always gets hurt. A bullet crashing through the roof, hitting some poor child lying in bed or someone sitting in their living room watching Dick Clark.

Of course, the cell phone is in the van being recharged. I'm so damned efficient. I look over at the picnic table and wonder if I can pull myself up. When I lift my arms, they hurt so bad I don't even bother trying. John is sitting on the ground, talking to himself.

I hiss at him. "John, I need you to be okay right now. Come on. Let's try to get over to the van. Can you move very well?"

He takes a long, pained breath. "I don't know."

"Can you get up? Try using the picnic table."

John slides himself over to the table. I watch him wince as he wraps his arms around the seat of the table. He's usually much more agile than me, but the fall took it out of him.

"I can't lift myself," he says.

"Put your back to the bench, maybe you can lift yourself that way."

John does what I say. "Now put pressure against the table and try to lift yourself with your hands. Now see if you can get some traction with your feet."

"Damn it," says John, almost getting his elbow up onto the bench. Then he collapses back into the dirt.

I am picturing how it could be done in my head, but we're both shook up and scared and dirty and tired. I want to cry, but it won't do any good. We'll still be here on the ground when I'm done bawling.

John hurts his back trying to do it again. I decide that it's my turn. I know I won't be able to lift myself up onto the picnic table, but I look over at the steps that flip out from the Leisure Seeker when you open the side door. It's about fifteen feet from where I am, so I steel myself for the long rough scoot over there.

"What are you doing?" says John.

"I'm going to get over to the door of the van, see if I can get in that way."

John grunts. But I can't tell if it's a "That's a good idea" grunt or a "You're out of your mind" grunt.

It takes me a good fifteen minutes to get halfway there. I lift, I scoot. I lift, I scoot. I am literally moving an inch at a time. The ground is hard here, so very hard, so many stones and pebbles biting into my hands and fanny. I'm sweating pretty bad now and it doesn't take long before it's in my eyes. This is the problem with having almost no hair—sweat goes straight down into your eyes. As I stop and wipe under my glasses with my filthy hands, I remember something from a guidebook, how we are in what the Mexicans called the "bad country." All the rock formations caused by black lava, with tinges of red that was supposed to be the blood of an awful monster slain by some gods of war. I don't know why I remember these things, but I can't help it.

The bad country indeed. I'm afraid the black earth is already tinged with the blood of this fat old broad. It's certainly getting no softer as I shrimp my way to the van. I'm numb from all this scraping, but for once I'm glad I've got this big rump to protect myself from the ground. This would hurt a lot more if I were one of those bony, rail-thin, smoked-for-a-hundred-years old crones. But then, if I was one of them, I could probably stand up.

John has given up and laid his head against the bench of the picnic table.

"John, why don't you start heading over here yourself? If I can get up a little bit, maybe you can help."

He lifts his head up from the bench, nods, then lays it back down, lulled to sleep by the whirr of the projector. I'm on my own.

Something happens when you're stuck on the ground in the near-dark, scared to death, not sure if you're ever going to stand up again, wondering what kind of shape you'll be in when they find you here in the morning. This is what happens: time stretches, pulls and folds itself over, then stretches itself again like Turkish Taffy that's been in your pocket all day. Right now, I have no idea if we've been on the ground for two hours or twenty minutes.

I keep scooting, nothing else to do. John is asleep by the bench. He will wake up wondering what he's doing on the ground. He will blame me for it, I'm sure of it. I get blamed just because I'm the only person around to blame. That's what will happen. He will awaken in a foul mood, thinking I've pushed him to the ground. He will yell at me.

Ow. Ow. Ow. I keep scooting. I hear that damn coyote again. If he comes here, thinking he's got an easy meal, he will be wrong. He will find what he thinks is a big fat buffet, but he won't think that for long. He will find a fight. I fought two men yesterday, so I'm not afraid of a coyote. I will kill him with my hands.

This is not where we are supposed to die.

After three breathers, cutting my hand on a piece of glass, crushing a large bug that I first think is a scorpion, but turns out to be a cicada or something, I'm finally at the steps of the van. They are small aluminum flip-down steps, very narrow, much too narrow for my wide beam, but I know they are sturdy because they are what we use to step into the van. Best of all, they are only a couple of inches from the dirt.

I back myself up to the lowest step, feel it with my wrists, which are mostly numb by this time. I take a hard breath and lift. I'm shaking, but I manage to raise myself onto the step. The narrow sides dig deep into my fanny, but at least I'm able to stay put. My tailbone feels secure on the step. It's such a relief just to be above the ground, I want to rest for about a half hour, but I don't. I grip the sides of the tiny steps and try to pull myself up again. This time, I can push ever so slightly with my heels as well. I make it up to the second step, but my butt does not feel as secure as it did on the first step. I shift my hands up farther, above the second step, and kick hard into the dirt with my heels. I'm so exhausted by this time, the tears are pouring from my eyes, but if I don't do this, we're going to be on the ground all night. I don't know if we can survive that.

I push hard and make it to the third step. I'm sitting on my hands now and it hurts. I pull one hand out, then the other, taking care not to lose my balance. I'm shaking so badly now, I don't know what to do.

"John!" I yell to him, as loudly as I can. I realize that I have not been yelling loudly enough, for fear of waking others. There's no one around. If there was, they could help us.

"John! Goddamn it!" I scream this time and it rouses him slightly. I see the head rise from the bench, then fall back down.

I search the ground around me. There are stones in the dirt, like the kind that have made my snail's journey so hard on my hands. I pick up three of the marble-sized rocks along with a handful of dust. My hands are so filthy now, I don't even care anymore. I chuck a stone at John and miss. I throw another one and miss again. I throw another, much harder, and this one hits home. John gets it in the side of the noggin. I'm ashamed to say that I'm rather pleased. There is a click as it connects, at least partly, with the earpiece of his glasses.

"Ow!" says John. "What the hell?"

"John! Get over here and help me get up these steps." Why am I doing this? It will take him at least a half hour to get over here. I just don't see why I have to do this by myself. I throw another rock at John and it hits him in the leg.

"Aah! Quit it! Quit hitting me." John rises slightly, clutching at the picnic table bench. Quickly, I grab more stones and keep tossing them at him.

"Would you stop it? You're hurting me."

I don't say a damned thing. I keep throwing rocks at my husband. It's angering him just enough for him to forget how feeble he is. He drags himself to his knees. I land a quarter-sized rock right in his ribs. He yowls and grabs at the top of the picnic table, lifts himself up all the way, groaning. I didn't think we would do it this way, but this will do.

"Get your ass over here and help me up," I say to him.

"Go to hell."

"John, please. I dragged myself all the way here just so I could get you up."

"I'm going to bed," he says, rubbing his eye with a filthy finger.

"You can't get in the van until you help me up."

I watch him make his way toward me. He shifts and veers a little bit, probably unsteady from being on the ground for so long. But as he approaches me, his gait is better, his stride stronger, the way it usually is. Tonight was just a bad night for him. I just needed to wake him up and annoy him enough for adrenaline to take over.

He unplugs the extension cord at the van outlet and the projector clicks off. John steps back toward the door. Something in his eyes changes as he towers over me.

"You're all dirty," he says, looking at me no longer with anger, but with tenderness.

"Help me up, John," I say.

John grabs one of the large metal handles he installed years ago on both sides of the door, leans forward and I reach out for him to pull me up, but instead, he bends down farther. He kneels at my feet and starts to tie my shoe. I have a hard time tying my shoes and often he has to do it for me. It's hardly what I'm concerned with at the moment, but I'm not going to stop him if he feels the need.

John ties a sloppy but secure bow on my dirty SAS orthopedic.

"Thank you, John," I say to my husband.

He smiles. "Hell, honey, you do all kinds of things for me."

John leans forward and kisses me on the lips. I can feel the cracks in them, the dry skin, but they feel fine just the same. I put my hand on his bristly face. Then he grabs my arm at the elbow and pulls me from the steps.

I'm up. We're not dead yet. My legs are throbbing, but they are steady enough to support me as I turn and grab the handle on the other side of the door with both hands. I pull my foot up onto the first tiny step, then the other foot. After a moment, I make it up to the next step.

"Wait a second," says John. He starts brushing the dirt off my backside.

"We're going to be out here all night if you try to sweep off my entire rear end," I say, too tired to even laugh.

"Hush," he says, patting, rubbing away.

So I hush and let him brush me off. Before long, I start

to feel more relaxed. My legs stop quivering. My breathing returns to normal. I did not expect a brush-down to soothe me so, but it does. John's touch hasn't changed through the years, still gentle, though his hands are toughened, stiffened, knobbed, and spotted with age, like everything else on our bodies. I experience a twinge of desire for him, through all the discomfort, through all the fear, through all the fatigue. I stand there on the steps, clutching the grip with both hands. I close my eyes.

We don't wake up until 1:35 in the afternoon the next day. It's then, when I open my eyes, that I feel as if I've gone ten rounds with Rocky Graziano. There are tears in my eyes before I even open them. It's discomfort, certainly, but also the other thing, the knowing. And the discomfort only brings you closer to that.

Before we went to sleep, I took all my meds, including two little blue pills, then gave John three extra-strength Tylenol and a Valium. I locked the door from the inside. There were no late-night visits to the bathroom, no disturbances, no episodes with John. Exhaustion trumps all disease. For the moment, the body minds only its most immediate need. The rest are left to sit in the corner, unaccustomed to the lack of attention.

I can't decide if we should try to keep moving today or stay put to rest. I think of Kevin, always the cautious one, saying to me, "Mom, if you feel tired or shaky, take it easy. That's when accidents occur. Everything always happens at once." He's right, too. Even when you're at your usual level of misery, you can maintain a certain stability. You're operating from a familiar place. But when you're extra scared or fatigued or discomfortable, some other bad thing is bound to happen. The past two days confirm this theory: a flat tire, a stickup, and a bad fall. The Morton Salt girl had it right. When it rains, it damn well pours.

Yet part of me needs to carry on, to trudge forward and shake hands with our grubby destiny. Though I know that it is not to be trusted, that destiny, with his loud plaid polyester suit, his halitosis, his cubic zirconium pinkie ring. Soon enough, we will stumble into his realm where he will heartily slap us on our backs with a meaty dampish paw, smile at us with nicotine teeth and promise us—*this fate here? That's the best one on the lot.*

Inertia makes the decision for me. I fall back into a semiconscious state. Around 3:30, John has an accident in bed. This is the first time that this has happened. The warmth seeps toward me, snaps my eyes open. At least it gets us out of bed. My first instinct is to yell at him, but I know it was an accident. Besides, I'm too tired to get mad. I do have to get those sheets off the bed. After I head for the bathroom myself.

When I come out, John has stripped down and is trying to tug a pair of different pants over his pissy drawers. There's other stuff on the drawers, too, but I'll spare you a description.

"John, you have to change your underwear."

"Ah, shut up," he says to me.

He can't pull up the pants because he's sore from last night. "Go into the bathroom and wash up. You *stink*."

"No, I don't. I'm fine." He keeps tugging.

This not washing has been a problem for some time. I'm fed up with it. "All right then. Let me help you," I say. "Here, just step out of them."

He stops struggling with the pants. "Why?"

"It'll be easier. We'll get you set right up."

John lets the pants fall to the floor and steps out of them. I reach over to our little junk drawer and pull out the pair of scissors he uses to trim the bread bag ends. Since I'm behind him, he can't see me snip through the waistband of his shorts. By the time he realizes what I'm doing, I'm down to the hem. I let them fall on the floor.

"Goddamn it. What the hell are you doing?"

"I'll have a new pair for you in a minute." I scuttle over to our cardboard clothes chest as fast as my throbbing legs can carry me and snatch a pair of fresh shorts. Then I grab a bar of soap and run two washcloths under warm water. Meanwhile, John is trying to pull the pants on over his bare ass.

"Just a second," I say. "Sit down. Then we can get the pants on." He parks his butt on our table with his thing just staring up at me. I rub soap onto one of the washcloths and hand it to him. "Here. Wash yourself off."

He grumbles, but he does it. It's nowhere near a good job, but it helps. While he does that, I strip the bed. The mattress is vinyl covered, so it just needs to be wiped down. Then I take the washcloth, the crusty shorts, the old pants, and the sheets and put them in a garbage bag to be thrown away. Time to start shedding things.

John is just barely able to get the clean shorts up over his knees and over his rump. I take the other washcloth and wipe down his face and neck. Soon, he starts to enjoy his French bath, telling me how good it feels. He always hates the idea of a bath, but once you get him clean, he feels a lot better. I spray him head to toe with Right Guard, then we wrestle on clean Sansabelts and a loud Hawaiian shirt that he picks out. By then, his mood is changed.

"I feel great."

"I'm so glad," I say, settling onto one of the benches along our table. "Because I'm exhausted."

"Let's get going," says John.

I watch as he trims the bread wrapper with the scissors that I just used to cut off his filthy skivvies. I'm too tired to stop him. "Let me get cleaned up, then we'll talk it over."

An hour and a half later, after counting my bruises, rinsing my abrasions, my own French bath, various ablutions, and a few close calls (the advantage of our tiny RV bathroom: you couldn't fall if you wanted to—not enough room), I'm also ready. The problem is, I don't know what I'm ready for. By the time we take our meds (plus a little blue for me) with a small meal of oatmeal, dried fruit, toast, and tea, it's 5:07 in the afternoon.

"Come on, let's go," says John, searching for his keys.

I look out the back door and see indentations in the dirt

where we were rolling around last night. "Yes," I say. "Let's get the hell out of here."

Good riddance to this bad country.

"What day is it?" John asks me after miles of silence and empty road.

"For God's sake," I say, peeved. At home, John is constantly asking what day it is and it drives me crazy. The kids buy him calendars for his birthday, so he'll stop asking them when they come over. But calendars don't help. How can you tell what day it is when you don't what month it is? Or what year?

"It's, it's—" As I stammer, I realize that I have absolutely no idea what day it is either. "It's Sunday," I say, because it feels like a Sunday to me.

"Oh," says John, satisfied.

"John, for right now, why don't we just see if we can make it to the Continental Divide?"

"Sure, okay."

He doesn't care. I think he's just happy to be driving. Actually, so am I. There are still a few hours of daylight left. We'll just see where we end up.

"Let's just take us a Sunday drive, John. What do you say?"

John nods.

We make it to the Continental Divide in nothing flat. All my life I have heard of it, but never really knew what it was. Simply put, it is the highest point of all Route 66 and the point at which rainfall divides. From this point, rainwater to the east drains into the Atlantic, water to the west drains into the Pacific. I read this all aloud to John, who grumbles as if he's known it and already forgotten it five or six times over.

The sun is lowering now, getting in our eyes. I pull out my jumbo sunglasses, though I believe it is not that long till sunset. I suppose common sense would dictate that we stop for the night, but I don't think either of us wants to, especially after only driving such a short time.

I stuff the guidebook in the fabric pocket of the door for safekeeping. "Okay, John, now let's see if we can make it to Gallup."

"Okay."

We should stop for the night, but I don't want to. After yesterday's goings-on, I figure we can do anything we want. All bets are off. Right now, I just want to watch the red sandstone cliffs shift, change colors, and grow more vivid as the sun liquefies. The vastness of the mesas, the stillness of all this stone soothes my wretched body, makes me feel part of the earth. The angling light reveals the character of the rock, how every inch is mottled and etched with time. I look at my arm, run my fingers across the million tiny folds that cover my skin like endless lines of faded calligraphy. There's something written in both places, but I can't read either.

Along the road, there are a few trading posts, some still

open, even at this time of day, but most long out of business. I spy an old Whiting Brothers Gas Station, its sign collapsing into the dust. The windows are all busted out and there's a giant bush growing where the pumps once stood. Those Whiting boys had dozens of gas stations in the West decades ago; now they're all gone or looking like this one.

I roll down the window, enjoying the caress of the air as it grows soft and cool, mellowing the day's swelter. I have always loved the feel of wind in my face, but love even more the sound of it rushing past my ears, blocking all else, creating a blur of noise.

Next to me, John seems content, not at all disoriented by the movement of the sun. He is focused on the road, occasionally checking the side-view mirror, not saying anything until after he takes a swig of flat Pepsi from a quarter-filled bottle he finds in his cup holder.

"Boy, am I sore today," he says, our night in the dirt completely forgotten.

"Yeah, me, too," I say. "Must be the weather."

It is near dark by the time we reach Gallup, but you can hardly tell from all the neon. For a mile or two, with all the motels and signs, it feels like Las Vegas when we visited it in the '60s, before all the casinos were crowded together, when there was still space between them, a sense of desert. Tonight, the neon signs glow warm and shimmery in the cobalt night:

BLUE SPRUCE LODGE
Lariat Lodge
ARROWHEAD LODGE
RANCH KITCHEN
MOTEL El Rancho

The last is a beautiful old hotel where lots of movie stars stayed, everyone from Humphrey Bogart to Hepburn and Tracy. Errol Flynn rode his horse into the bar. I've heard that it's a classy old joint, but we won't be stopping there tonight.

Before long, Gallup becomes a city. As we follow the old alignment, it takes us past a beautiful old theater called the El Morro. The marquee is dark tonight.

"How are your eyes holding out, John?"

"They're okay."

Just then, a little hopped-up Japanese car zips up next to us. It's bright yellow with loud, high-pitched exhaust pipes and a big air spoiler on the back. I look over at the driver to see who's making all the racket. I'm surprised to see a teenage girl there. After a moment, she gooses it and whinnies on past. On her back window, there's a sticker:

NO FEAR

I think, *good girl*.

Nine

ARIZONA

This is an evening of bad judgment.

It has been many, many years since we've driven through the night. And for us to choose a stretch of desert to do it in is certainly a foolish idea. The kids would be terrified if they knew we were doing this. It's exactly the sort of thing they're having nightmares about. But the fact is, I don't care and John doesn't know any better. It's just another long highway in front of him.

When we were younger, it wasn't uncommon for us, in a sudden end-of-vacation rush to get home, to drive twenty, twenty-four, even thirty hours straight. It was a punishing thing to do, a kind of trance to which you had to give yourself over. Deaf with fatigue, you thought of nothing beyond the road, beyond the quivering bright scoops of your headlights.

On those nights when we surrendered to that madness, the miles would hiss past with a jagged, frazzled rhythm. We would stop for gasoline every half hour, it seemed, greet a new state every hour. Our senses were heightened to the point where we'd hear every seam of the asphalt, every click of the odometer.

John would drink so much coffee his stomach would creak and growl. He would chain-smoke Galaxy cigarettes and scream at the kids. Yet he kept driving, guzzling gas station mud, crunching down Tums with every cup. Out of boredom, I would dole out whatever was left in our cooler—lunch meats, warm pops, fruits from roadside stands, foods edging brown and green. After twenty or more hours, our car took on the smell of kitchen, bedroom, and bathroom all in one. Our whole family's eyes became accustomed to the dark. Through glass smudged with stale breath, gas stations glowed and throbbed in the empty night, motel neon smeared red-orange trails; the reflection of our high beams in the highway signs flash-blinded us as we shot past.

The only thing that could move us to damage ourselves in such a way was to get home. There would come a time after twelve or thirteen days of near-solid travel that all you wanted was to be in your own house. Travel was wonderful, travel was glorious. *See the USA in your Chevrolet!* But what you wanted more than anything right then, was simply to sleep in your own bed, eat in your own kitchen, sit on your own toilet. You wanted to stop seeing the world. You wanted to see *your* world. So we would drive.

The all-night journeys were never planned. We would never intend to drive so ridiculously long and far. We would get one of those "good" days under our belt—six hundred miles or so—then we'd suddenly get fussy, unable to find a decent campground in our AAA guides or from the billboards along the road. We didn't want to stay in a motel. We'd already spent enough money after two weeks on the road. (We were getting close enough to home to realize that we'd have to pay those credit card bills soon enough.) We'd say, *Let's just drive a little longer. See how far we can go before we have to stop.*

So we would drive. A little bit farther. A little bit farther. Twilight would come, arc over us, a lump of sun dissolving in our wake, turning our rear window into color television. Then night would settle in, gather around us, cozylike, an afghan of stars. It was a relief to our eyes after the cruel shifting beauty of sunset. After a while, the kids would even stop whining and complaining and settle down. They were as anxious to get home as we were. Then without even trying, it would be 11:00 P.M., way too late to stop for the night. We knew what we were doing by then. Too late to turn back. *Drive, drive.* We were heading toward something, a place we wanted, needed to be.

Tonight, John and I are smack in the middle of the Navajo nation. A gritty breeze buffets the half-open window. Along the highway, I see forked silhouettes of cacti, glints of rubbed rock and dynamited stone, darkened empty trading posts with signs that advertise INDIAN JEWELRY AT SUPER PRICES! I'm scared to be out here in the dark, but it's no longer a fear that I can take seriously. It's all starting to feel like one of the rides at Disneyland. Of course, this may have something to do with all the discomfort pills I'm popping. It's the only way I can operate now. I guess it's happened: I've officially become a hophead. Frankly, I thought it would be more fun than this. I still have no idea why the kids love the dope so much.

I keep a close eye on John as he drives. He reminds me of the John of forty years ago (without a cigarette between his fingers), eyes trained on the road, very alert, not even yawning. I see no traces of the "highway hypnosis" that they used to warn us motor travelers against. *(Chew gum! Open the windows! Sing along with the radio!)* We are both too awake, one of us too aware.

John and I are tethered to the interstate tonight. No side trips in search of the pink concrete of the original 66. At night, there's just too much chance that we would get good and lost. This way, all we have to do is stay on I-40 and keep moving for as long as we can. Yes, it's a shame that we're driving through the Painted Desert in the dark, but tonight is special. We need to get to our destination soon. I can tell.

"I'm going to play some music, John," I say, fumbling with our bulky case of remaining eight-track tapes. We used to have a lot more, but our stereo has devoured them over the years. I find one called *Provocative Percussion* by Enoch Light & the Light Brigade and plug it into the player. "Blues in the

Night" comes on way too loud, scaring the crap out of both of us. John must have accidentally turned it up when it was off. I turn it down and it sounds all right for a moment, but then the music starts to warble. The woodwinds are pulled thin, and the plucky guitar notes ring flat, but I don't care. I need sound. I don't want to be alone with my thoughts. I don't like my thoughts anymore. They are not to be trusted.

My mouth is so dry. I take a sip from one of the bottles of emergency water. I look over at John and he looks back with the emptiness in his eyes, but also with affection. He whistles along with the music and taps on the steering wheel.

"Hello there, young lady," he says, smiling at me.

I turn down "Fascinating Rhythm," which is so chipper and cheery that it's almost too much to handle, even with the distortion slowing it down.

"Do you know who I am, John?"

"Sure," he says, smiling, faking it for me.

"Who am I then?"

"Don't you know who you are?"

He's tried this before. "Sure, I know," I say. "I just want to know if you know."

"I know."

"Then who am I?"

"You're my lover."

"That's right." I lay my hand on his knee. "So what's my name?"

He smiles again. His lips move, but nothing comes out. "'S Wonderful" comes on the stereo, sounding like it's being played on a tuba.

"What?" I say.

"Is it Lillian?"

I take my hand away. Son of a bitch. *Lillian?* "Who the hell is Lillian?"

He says nothing. I know he's confused, but I don't really care. "You heard me. Who's Lillian?"

"I don't know."

"You don't know?" I smack him in the arm. "You just said Lillian was your lover."

"I don't know."

I don't know what this means, but I want to strangle him. When I used to ask John if he'd ever step out on me, he always used to say that he wouldn't be here if he wasn't faithful. Now I'm wondering. "Who's Lillian?" I repeat.

"I'm married to Lillian."

"No, you're not. You're married to me. I'm Ella."

"I thought your name was Lillian."

"We've been married practically sixty years. You can't remember my goddamned name?"

"I thought—"

"Oh shut up," I say, punching the off button, then yanking the cartridge from the stereo. The music sputters out as tape spills from the slot.

John sighs, leans back in his seat, and sulks. I do the same.

━━

The miles pass silently. The moon rises, about three-quarters full, revealing vague clues of the Painted Desert: silver glimpses of veiny hills, ridged brick-striped plateaus, and puffy glow balls of scrub. It's a relief to get off the freeway in Holbrook for gas. I recall that there's something to see here, but don't feel like looking in my books. Then just inside the city limits, in front of a rock shop, I see a gathering of gigantic prehistoric creatures—dinosaurs, brontosauruses, stegosauruses—all colors and sizes, loitering along the road between scattered chunks of petrified wood.

"Well, look at that," I say to John, though I'm still ticked at him.

"There's Dino," he says, brightly.

The tallest one does look like the old Sinclair dinosaur. Towering over the others, neck swanned, the stone reptile peers curiously at us from the side of the road. He knows his own kind when he sees them.

We turn a corner through this deserted burg and pass down Main Street. That's when I remember what's in Holbrook and it ain't the dinosaurs. Before long, I can see the neon blazing green against the desert horizon.

WIGWAM MOTEL
Have you slept in a wigwam lately?

Behind the sign and the office, there is a glowing half circle of shiny white teepees, each ringed with crimson rickrack, a single spotlight bright at the crown.

"John. Do you remember staying here on our first trip to Disneyland?"

"We never stayed there," says John.

"Yes, we did. It was small inside, but it was comfy. The kids loved it."

It crosses my mind to pull in there, knock off for the night and sleep in one of those concrete wigwams again for old times' sake, but we are getting so far into Arizona, making steady time, that I don't want to stop. Besides, I remember our slides of the inside of our wigwam, the dinky log furniture, the cramped bathroom. It was tiny. We might as well just sleep in the van.

Down the street, we stop for gas, use the credit card, slide in and out of the restrooms. We don't speak to a soul.

A dozen miles in the velvet darkness. Briefly on 66, we pass a place with a giant jackrabbit standing sentry in the parking lot. It gives me the heebie-jeebies. The dinosaurs were much more friendly looking.

Later, back on I-40 near Winslow, a roadrunner zips across our path. I remember these little birds from previous trips. Frankly, I remember them being faster than this one. John never even saw it as it crossed the beam of our headlights. I saw it only for an instant. When we hit the poor thing, there was barely a noise to speak of, just a *thup,* as if we had run over a milk carton.

"What was that?" said John.

"I think we hit a bird," I say, my voice splintering. "A road-runner."

"A what?"

"A *roadrunner.* You know, like what Wile E. Coyote used to chase?" I feel bad for the little creature. It all happened so fast I didn't have a chance to make a peep. This seems like a bad omen. Suddenly, I feel like one of those sailors who must wear an albatross around his neck after killing it. I try to think about something else.

The frantic part of my discomfort is gone now, and I feel less in a panic to get to Disneyland. A quick check of my books tells me that we have another six hundred miles to the end of the road, then another fifty to Anaheim. I was a fool to think we could make it there tonight.

It's almost 10:30. John keeps yawning and rubbing his face.

"John, do you want a Pepsi?" I say. "I think we have one somewhere."

He shakes his head. "Not thirsty."

John could drink tea, coffee, and pop all day long, but here in the middle of the desert, he's not thirsty.

"John, do you want to stop for the night?"

He says nothing.

"You want to drive a little more?"

"Yeah."

"Why don't we head for Flagstaff and get something to eat?" I say, not knowing if anything will be open this late, but we'll try.

We get to Wendy's just as it's about to close for the night. The voice of the woman at the drive-thru is the first that we've heard all night besides our own. We sit in the parking lot and watch the sky and mountains grow brighter as they switch the signs off, then moments later, the dining room lights. The moon and a nearby streetlamp allow us just enough light to see each other inside the van.

John chews his hamburger intently. I suck hard at the straw in my Frosty, but nothing happens. Through the windshield, the world tonight feels to me like an alien place. I haven't been out driving at this time of night in many years, much less in an unfamiliar area. These are the things that scare you as you get older. You understand night all too well, all its attendant meanings. You try to avoid it, work around it, keep it from entering your house. Your weary, but ornery body tells you to stay up late, sleep less, keep the lights on, don't go into the bedroom—if you have to sleep, sleep in your chair, at the table. Everything is about avoiding the night. Because of that, I suppose that I should be scared out here in the dark, but I am finally past that, I think.

John clears this throat as he finishes off his single with cheese. He licks catsup off his finger and glances at my burger on the console, only two bites taken out of it.

"Go ahead," I say.

John picks up the burger and digs in. I pop the top of my Frosty and go at it with a plastic spoon. The ice cream cools my parched throat and calms my stomach.

Every once in a while a car hisses past.

John stops chewing. He puts my hamburger down, wipes his lips with a napkin, places his hand on my thigh. "Hi lover," he says to me, completely forgetting what happened before.

He knows who I am. He knows that I am the one person who he loves, has always loved. No disease, no person can take that away.

The lobby of the Flagstaff Radisson is lovely. I wonder if they've just recently renovated the place as I wheel on up to the check-in counter. Tonight I have broken out the You-Go, my rolling walker. It's got lockable hand brakes, a basket for my purse, and a seat in case I get tired, all with a jazzy "candy apple red" (as Kevin calls it) paint job. We're at that point where I need more support to keep me steady on my feet. We cannot afford any more falls.

"What kind of rooms do you have? Do you have something nice?" I ask the desk clerk. This is not like me. I'm more likely to ask, "What's the cheapest room in the joint?"

The clerk, a Mexican fellow with a receding hairline and

a postage stamp of hair under his lip, looks up from his book and stares dolefully at me. According to his nametag, his name is "Jaime."

"I've got a standard double, nonsmoking, and a suite, also nonsmoking," he says. The accent gives his words a roundness that's pleasant to my ear.

"We'll take the suite," I say, tired of scrimping.

"It's one-twenty-five a night, plus tax," he says.

I gasp. "Jesus, I don't want to buy the place, I just want to sleep here."

Jaime shrugs at me.

"I'm sorry." I hand him our Visa. I decide that we're going to give that little bugger a workout in the next few days. But being a spendthrift is going to take some getting used to. I've never paid that much for a hotel room in my life.

As he runs our card through the machine, there's a long uncomfortable silence.

"Excuse me," I say. "How do you pronounce your name?"

He eyeballs me for a moment, then he says, "Hi-Meh."

"Oh, like the Jewish pronunciation?"

"Not really, ma'am."

"Well, I'm glad I didn't call you Jamie."

There's a flicker of amusement in his eyes. "Me, too."

We leave our van in the handicapped space. Jaime gets our overnight bags (packed special for when we stay in hotels) and takes us on up to our room. I'm pleased. It's done in shades of gold and beige, all looking very new. There's a living room and a bedroom and I try not to think about all this space that we don't need. I try not to kick myself for my extravagance. I tell myself to hell with it, stop worrying, live a little.

"That's the minibar," says Jaime, walking around, pointing at things. "You've also got a DVD player and a stereo. Over here's the kitchenette area. There's the coffeepot and a snack basket. All the prices are listed on that sheet."

"This is a nice room," says John. "Can we afford it?"

I turn to him. "Hush, John. Of course we can." I smile at Jaime, then I look in my purse for a tip.

He holds his hand up as if to say it's not necessary. "Enjoy your stay," he says as he exits.

I wheel the You-Go over to the stereo, turn it on, and look for a station that doesn't make my head hurt. I'm still craving noise to keep the thoughts at bay. I find one of those smooth saxophone stations and leave it there. Then I steer over to the minibar. "Let's have a cocktail, John. It'll help us to sleep."

"All right."

The minibar has tiny bottles of Crown Royal, but no sweet vermouth, so we have to improvise. After I pour out our drinks, I get a packet of Sweet'n Low from my purse and sprinkle half in each drink, stir it with my finger. Some considerate soul has also filled the tiny ice cube tray so we're all set. I don't once look at the price sheet. Maybe being a wastrel will be easier than I thought.

John and I sit down at the little table in the living room to enjoy our cocktails. He looks around at the room and whistles. "Wow, what is this place?"

"It's our fancy hotel room. Pretty classy, huh?"

"I'll say," he says as he raises his glass to me. "This is the life."

"What's left of it," I say, raising my glass to meet his.

Two manhattans later, John is on the bed in the other room, in his clothes, snoring like a buzz saw. I'm hoping he won't have another accident. I'm sitting here, thinking about putting the TV on, but I just can't seem to get myself to do it. My head is swimming, maybe low blood sugar, but most likely booze and pills. I finally understand that expression *feeling no pain*. That's okay. That's how we dope fiends operate.

I wake up with my husband for the second morning in a row. Instead of sleeping in the comfy chair, as I would normally do, at the last moment I wheeled myself into the bedroom to sleep with John. There are no bladder accidents as far as I can see or feel or smell, and when I open my eyes after a few furtive hours of what might be called sleep, but is really more like switching through a thousand different channels of cable TV all of which are devoted to moments in one's life, I am rewarded.

"Good morning, Ella," says John to me, his eyes clear and glistening.

"Hi, John."

"You sleep good?" He plucks his glasses from the night-stand and puts them on.

"Not really. How about you?"

"I slept like a rock. I feel swell."

"I'm glad."

He looks around the room, eyes wide. "Jeez, the place looks great. You clean up?"

I'm amazed. For once in John's mind, home isn't some run-down trailer park or crummy motor lodge. Finally, home is a four-star hotel. That's what I've been waiting to hear.

"Yes, I did clean up," I say, touching his cheek. "John, do you remember when we went to Lake George in New York?"

"Did the kids go along?"

"Not that time. Cindy was married by then and Kevin was old enough to stay home alone. We went on our own."

John grins. "I remember one thing about Lake George. We had the room with the hot tub? And we skinny-dipped."

I smile, too. "We were both a lot skinnier then."

John looks in my eyes. The old John looks in my eyes, cocks his head, then he kisses me. He kisses me harder than I can remember him kissing me for a long time. We kiss like a man and woman kiss, not like two old people who call each other Mom and Dad. But when he kisses me, there is a sourness to his mouth that makes my stomach flutter and rotate and I can feel the booze from last night churning, along with all the dope, wrenching those bites of hamburger from my guts up into my throat. Up it comes, a brief gusher of acid. Not much really, but it burns like hell. I pull myself from John just in time to vomit on the floor next to the bed.

"Ella. What's wrong?" says John.

I have to wait to turn back to him, just to make sure that

I don't have another geyser coming. I am panting now, trying not to do it too loudly, so as not to alarm John. I'm not doing a very good job.

"Ella!" He gets up to go to the bathroom. "I'm going to get you a glass of water." After a breath, I turn around to watch where he goes. He finds the bathroom right away, no problem. I suppose if you think a place is home, you probably know where the bathroom is. He comes back with a glass of water.

"Drink this. See if it makes you feel any better."

"Is it cold?"

"Lukewarm. It's okay. Drink it."

I drink the warm water. At first, I think I'm going to puke it back up, but it stays down. The nausea passes.

"Feel better?"

I nod. I like having him be so concerned and worried about me like this. It's been so long since he's taken care of me and not the other way around.

"What do you think made you sick?"

"Just last night's dinner," I say. "I guess it upset my stomach."

He doesn't remember last night or what we ate or anything about it. He lies down next to me again and we don't speak for a few minutes.

Still a bit shaky, I get up, fill the ice bucket with warm water, grab the little spray can of Lysol I carry in my over-night bag, gather our remaining towels, and try to clean up my mess.

Though I could've easily stayed in that beautiful hotel another day, I knew that we needed to keep going. I called the front desk to get help with our bags. Checkout was at 11:00 A.M., but I laid on the old lady charm ("Oh, I'm so sorry. We just plain forgot. It happens when you get to our age.") and got us out of there without paying for another night. I was tempted to tell them to use a little something extra on the carpeting next to the bed, but I decided we should just get while the getting was good.

We reconnect with 66 in Flagstaff's "Historic Railroad District." Before long, it turns into the frontage road for the freeway. Last night, I was frantic about getting to Disneyland, thinking that we should take the fast road all the way, but today I've decided that we'll be all right, at least for a while. I'm feeling better after some sleep, such as it was. We won't be visiting the Grand Canyon, though, I'm afraid.

So instead of turning right on Highway 64, which would take us to the canyon, we turn left for a quick jaunt though the town of Williams, just for old times' sake. It's a bit down at the heels these days, but I'm happy to see that Rod's Steak House is still around. We stopped for a steak there once on our way to the canyon. Their jumbo brown-and-white steer statue is still on the sidewalk in front. That's their trademark. Even their menus are shaped like a big cow. Mentally, I add this to the list of giants that have revealed themselves to us here on the Mother Road.

About twenty miles down the road, we pass through a small town called Ash Fork, where I see—*ta-dah!*—a restaurant called the Route 66 Diner. We also spot a beauty salon called Desoto's with an old purple-and-white car on the roof. Why it's there, I do not know. Mostly we see long sunbaked lots filled with cut stone. We pass acre upon dusty acre of it— textured fieldstone, bleached fawn and silver, rough-hewn and chiseled flat. It's piled on skids, on the ground, even stacked vertically, its irregular shapes jutting upward like the skyline of a dozen cities crushed together. One of my books says that Ash Fork holds the dubious title of "Flagstone Capital of the World." One lot has nothing but huge, oversized steles. Two huge blank slabs in particular catch the glare of the sun, almost absorbing it, but not quite. The brightness is too much for my eyes, even with my sungoggles. I have to turn away.

John is quiet and I am thankful for it. I pick up the cellular phone and dial Kevin's number. He should be just getting home from work by this time.

"Hello?"

"Kevin. It's your mother."

"Mom. Thank God. Are you okay?"

He sounds so worried. I feel a jolt of guilt for making him suffer like this, but there's no choice. "We're fine, honey," I say, putting on an extra-cheery voice. "Everything's *great*."

God, am I a big fat liar.

Kevin's voice, usually a solid baritone, rises as he speaks. "Mom, Dr. Tomaszewski thinks you should come home immediately."

"Oh, does he?" I say. "Well, tell Dr. Tom to mind his own damn business."

"Mom, please," says Kevin, frantically. "You can't keep doing this."

"Kevin, I am tired of doing what everyone else thinks I should do."

Kevin takes a long breath. "Dr. Tom says if you don't come home, you're not going to last—"

"Damn it, Kevin, *stop it*." I'm screeching into the phone by this time. I did not call to get all upset. I take a breath myself, try to calm down. "Honey, this vacation is a good thing, it really is. We're having a real nice time."

"No, you guys are coming home. *I mean it*."

I'm surprised to hear this attitude from Kevin. He's usually not this way, especially with me. "No, Kevin. And I don't appreciate your tone."

"I don't care. We spoke to the State Police."

I am not pleased with my son. "Kevin Charles Robina, why would you go and do something like that?"

"We didn't know what else to do, Mom. That's why."

I can't see it, but I know he's got that mad, pouty look that he gets on his face when he defies me.

"Well, there's nothing they can do," I say brightly. "We haven't broken any laws. Your father has a legal driver's license."

Kevin says nothing. The police probably said the same thing to him. Being old is not against the law. Not yet, at least.

"Mom, we tracked your credit card. I know approximately where you are. I'm coming to get you guys."

"Don't you dare, Kevin. I *mean* it." I say this with all the maternal authority I can muster. "Now I want you to stop worrying. We're both just fine."

"I don't believe you."

I can hear his voice starting to crack. He's trying to be strong. John would always tell Kevin not to cry, not to be a big baby, but he couldn't help it. I would always say, *Stop yelling at him, John. He can't help it. He's just sensitive.*

"Sweetie, it doesn't matter if you believe me or not."

"If you come back, Mom, maybe you can get better." His voice is quivering and damp with tears now, a voice that's all too familiar to me.

"Dear," I say, suddenly exhausted, "now you're talking crazy."

The line cracks and I almost think I'm going to lose the connection, but then it comes back.

John turns to me. "Who are you talking to?"

"I'm talking to Kevin, our son."

"Hi, Kevin!" yells John, suddenly jolly. I hold the phone to John's ear. "How's my big boy?" he says. John listens for a second, then smiles. "Aw, we're fine. Talk to Mom."

"We have to go, Kevin," I say, once I'm back on the line. "Tell your sister we called."

A long pause. I hear my son blow his nose.

"Will you do that?" I ask.

Another pause. "Yes, Mom."

He says something else, but I can't make it out. His voice sounds far away. "We love you both," I say. "Remember that."

"Mom? I can't hear you."

"Kevin? Kevin? Are you there?" I pull the phone away from my ear, try to find a volume button on it. When I look at the dial, it says:

SIGNAL FADED

Well, I didn't need all this.

I think about something that happened when Kevin was over at the house a few years back, putting the storm window in the front door. He accidentally cut himself on the door hinge. It wasn't rusty, thank God, but it was sharp. He walked into the kitchen, blood dripping from his finger. As soon as I saw what happened, I jumped up and fetched a Band-Aid for him. I put a dab of antibiotic ointment on it then wrapped the Band-Aid around his finger, making it just tight enough. Then I squeezed his finger and, without thinking, gave it a little kiss. *That'll make it better*, I said. Then I looked up and saw a forty-four-year-old man. It had been decades since something like that had occurred between us, yet nothing had ever felt so familiar.

These are the things that squeeze the breath out of me when I remember them. Just when I start to think I'll be okay with what's happening, something like this pulls everything apart, leaves me shattered.

═══

We are both quiet for a while after the call. I try very hard to think about something else. "John, there's a place in Seligman that's supposed to have good chicken. How does that sound to you?"

"Nah."

I sigh. "They've got hamburgers, too."

"Now you're talking."

Good Lord. I don't know why I even bother. I've had so many hamburgers this trip, I'm about to start mooing.

When we reach Seligman, it looks to be yet another depressed little burg, then we get to Delgadillo's Snow Cap Drive-In. I read that it was supposed to be different, but I'm not quite prepared for how different it is.

"What the hell kind of crazy place is this?" says John.

"It's supposed to be fun," I say, but he's right, it looks crazy. Painted red and orange and blue and yellow, the place is cluttered with mismatched furniture, old gas pumps, banners, even an outhouse. An ancient flivver is parked next to the door, decorated with claxon horns, flags, plastic flowers, and twinkle lights. There are signs all over the place.

DEAD CHICKEN
CHEESEBURGERS WITH CHEESE
EAT HERE AND GET GAS
MERRY CHRISTMAS!
SORRY WE'RE OPEN

I consider forgetting the whole thing, but there's a tour bus parked in front of the place, so how bad can it be? Besides, we need a break. Maybe it'll be fun.

Inside, it isn't any less crazy. After getting laughed at by all the tour bus people on the patio for trying to get in through a door with a fake doorknob (John was not pleased), I wheel us into a room where the walls and ceiling are covered with calling cards, notes, postcards, and foreign money. It didn't look as clean as I would like, but maybe it was just all the stuff hanging there.

Behind the counter is a tanned man in his fifties, all eyebrows and teeth and brilliantined hair, smiling like he can't wait to talk to us. "LOOK!" he yells, then throws a candy bar on the counter.

John and I both look. LOOK is the name of the candy bar. I summon a polite smile. I hear laughing from the people in line behind us.

"What the *hell* is this place?" says John, in a tone that is not courteous.

It doesn't faze the counterman, whose laugh is somewhere between a yelp and a bark. "Our special today is chicken!" he says, swinging a big rubber hen.

"Don't wave that goddamn thing at me," says John.

I see the uneasiness in the face of the man behind the counter.

"John," I say, trying to smooth things out. "He's only joking. I think they do that here."

"This isn't McDonald's," hisses John. I watch the redness

217

spread across his forehead, down his cheeks. His upper lip twitches.

"Calm down, John." I avoid the stares of the folks behind us, a family with a little girl.

But he's riled up. "What the fuck kind of place did you take me to?" he roars, slamming his hand on the counter, palm down. The candy bar trembles.

The counterman is not smiling anymore. He looks shocked and scared. "Sir, you're going to have to leave."

"You shove it up your ass!" bellows John.

I grab John's arm and pull him toward the door. "I'm sorry," I say to the counterman. "He's not well." But there's no sympathy in the man's face, only hurt and anger. It looks like he could cry. We're making everyone cry today. John and Ella just out there spreading joy, that's us.

John just stares at him, then steers his death ray at me. Fast as I can roll, I push past the little girl, who is about seven, with short sandy hair, big ash-colored eyes, and a barrette with a cartoon cat head on it. Biting her lip, she looks at me pleadingly, not sure what's just happened.

"I'm sorry you had to hear that, honey," I say, trying to smile at her. She runs forward and pulls open the door for us. I touch her tender arm for a moment and keep moving. Out on the patio, the tour bus people are laughing, oblivious to the scandal that just occurred inside. I whisper to John, "We'll go somewhere else for lunch."

"Goddamn right we will," he snarls.

In the van, John is still muttering. I don't say anything.

218

I'm scared of him right now. I bury my head in one of my guidebooks. I read about the stretch of 66 ahead, from Mc-Connico to Topock, leading to California. By all accounts, it's the most authentic part of old 66 left—long stretches of isolated desert, ghost towns, roaming packs of hungry wild burros, loose gravel on the shoulders, and winding switchback canyon roads.

I direct us onto the interstate.

Ten

CALIFORNIA

We have arrived at our final state. After many hushed, tense miles, the sight of the Colorado River and WELCOME TO CALIFORNIA sign make me feel better, despite the fact that I am hellishly tired. We both are, I think. The time changes and crazy hours have caught up to us. The blazing heat doesn't help, not to mention the fact that the AC doesn't work at all anymore. And of course, we still have to travel with the windows partially open at all times because of the exhaust. Still, I haven't suffered all that much discomfort. My trusty little blue pills have seen to that. Ella the crazed dope addict strikes again.

"We're going to stay in a hotel tonight," I tell John, trying to sound assertive, though I'm still afraid of him after the episode at the Snow Cap.

"Sure. Good idea," he says, nice as you please.

We roll into the dreary outskirts of Needles. I will try not to be fussy about a motel, but I know I'll be miserable if we end up in a fleabag.

"John, there's a place over there. It says 'Vacancy.' Pull in."

Without a word, John pulls in. I open the door of the van and a big blast of hot desert air hits me and almost knocks me on my fanny, I swear.

John gets my You-Go and wheels it around. I plop my purse in the basket and we head on up to the lobby. As soon as I walk in, I smell something I don't like. I don't know if it's food or body odor or what, but I don't like it.

"Can I help you?" says the young woman at the desk.

"No, thank you," I say, turning around. John opens the door for me.

We go into three other hotels like this. I figure if a hotel can't even keep its lobby clean, how are the rooms going to be? It's almost 7:00 P.M. by the time we settle on the Best Western and I'm about ready to keel over. There is no one to help us with our bags, so I have to put mine on the You-Go, which makes it harder to push. Luckily, there's a handicap space right in front of the hotel by the lobby.

When I get into the room, there's a delivery menu from a restaurant down the street. I order us roast beef sandwiches and milk shakes, then take my meds and a little blue pill and flop into bed. By the time the food arrives, I feel much better. John turns on the TV while we eat. It isn't long before I fall asleep.

I dream of our old bungalow in Detroit. It's nice being there again. Everything is the same. I recognize our old Danish Modern dining room set from Hudson's, our old couch, I recognize the daisy pattern wallpaper that John hung in the kitchen. I can see the basement that John paneled and that I furnished with early American furniture from Arlens. I don't even remember looking at these things in the dream, but I know they are there.

In the dream, I'm sitting in Cindy's old room after she moved out to get married. We never really did anything with the room, but there was enough space for a television and a couple of old chairs. It's late at night and John is asleep upstairs. I'm with Kevin, who's about thirteen, and we're watching Johnny Carson. We were both night owls and we watched *The Tonight Show* every night. I missed having Cindy around the house so it was nice spending time with my son, even though he probably shouldn't have been staying up so late. But we both loved the comedians— Buddy Hackett, Bob Newhart, Shecky Greene, Alan King, Charlie Callas.

In the dream, we are watching Johnny do his Carnac the Magnificent routine where he dresses like a swami and holds an envelope to his forehead and divines the answers to the questions inside the envelope. Kevin and I are laughing at something Johnny says to Ed about a diseased yak in his sleeping bag.

It's a wonderful quiet little dream. Me just watching TV with my son in a room filled with old furniture. We're eating cheese crackers and laughing. The only odd part is the answer to one of Carnac's questions.

"Mickey Mouse, Donald Duck, and the Ayatollah Khomeini," Johnny says, holding the envelope to his turban.

Ed looks at Johnny and repeats, *"Mickey Mouse, Donald Duck, and the Ayatollah Khomeini."*

Carnac stares daggers at Ed, then he rips open the envelope and reads, "Who you'll meet at the Disneyland in hell."

I have no idea what time it is when the phone rings. I'm not even sure where it is that I'm sleeping. I try to look at the clock, but I don't have my glasses on. The phone rings and rings, just like at home because the kids know it takes us a long time to get to it. Finally, I manage to pick it up.

"Hello?"

"Mrs. Robina? This is Eric, the night clerk at the front desk. Um, your husband is down here and he, uh, seems a little confused."

"Is he all right?"

"He's fine. It's just that he's upset. First he went outside and stood by your van for a little while, came in, went back out there, then he came in asking me where his keys were. That's when I looked up what room he was in."

I take a breath, rub the sand from my left eye. At least he's okay.

"Now he keeps asking me where the coffee is. I told him that we don't have coffee until 6:30 A.M., but he insists we have it somewhere. He's getting perturbed."

"I'm terribly sorry," I say. "I'll be down there as soon as I can."

Thank God I remembered to take the keys away from him last night.

"Where were you?" says John, in the elevator back to our room.

I'm weaving over my You-Go, still woozy from being awakened so abruptly. "I was upstairs sleeping, John."

"I want to get going."

I lead us off the elevator to our room. "It's too early. Let's try to get a little more sleep, all right?"

"Let's get going."

"John, it's 4:30 in the morning. It's too early. We're going to get all screwed up."

I get John settled in with the TV and a little bag of potato chips from the snack basket. There's an old episode of *Cheers* on, which keeps him happy. I lie with him on the bed with my head propped up on the big mound of pillows we have constructed from every pillow in the joint. Needless to say, I can't sleep anymore. It's too soon for another pill. I consider a drink, but it's too close to morning.

The *Cheers* music comes on with the credits. John wipes his greasy fingers on his shirt. "Okay," he says. "Let's hit the road."

"John, it's too early. It's five in the morning."

"Aren't we getting an early start?"

"No, we're going to get some sleep. We paid a lot for this hotel room and I'd like to get some use out of it."

Two minutes later from John: "Okay, let's get going."

"Oh, the hell with it," I say. "Fine, let's get going."

Before we leave, I take a sponge bath in the bathroom, using all the towels and washcloths, cleaning everywhere I've been meaning to clean for the past week. God knows, I hope I haven't been one of those old ladies that goes around with her old lady smell. My aunt Cora was like that. People's eyes were watering after she left a room. I told myself I'd never be that way.

By the time we leave, the hotel room is an absolute shambles. I've never left a room like that in my life. I've always practically made the bed before I left, but not this time. For one thing, I'm not strong enough this morning. Besides, for what we paid for this room, they can jolly well clean up after us.

After we gas up the Leisure Seeker, we do indeed hit the road. The early start turns out to be a good idea since we're heading west out of Needles right through the Mojave on the original alignment of 66. Early is the best time to head through the desert.

We are the only people on the road when the sun begins to

rise. I sit in my captain's chair in the Leisure Seeker, a Styrofoam cup of tepid gas station coffee in my hand as I watch the
colors lift the night sky—violet evaporating to cherry pink,
charcoal vanishing to chalky blue. The stars fade as outlines
of spiky aloe and twined brush and jutting silver Sacramento
Mountains emerge upon the horizon as if an Ansel Adams
photograph were being developed before my eyes.

Maybe it's because we're close to the end of our trip that I'm
getting sentimental, but I feel as though I was supposed to see
this today. And John, in his madness, allowed it to happen.

I reach over and touch his arm. "Thank you."

John looks at me, worried.

It isn't long before the Mojave wears out its welcome. Once the
sun starts its brutal ascent, the landscape changes. Desolation
enters through the eyes and soon invades the vitals. I stare out
at naked mountains and empty dun-colored landscape. There
is brush everywhere, leached of color, large lifeless clouds of it
pluming the stamped-down earth. We keep passing a certain
type of cactus with long spiny branches that twist up from the
ground like arthritic fingers trying to hold on to something.
I remember from *The Grapes of Wrath* when Tom Joad called
this desert the bones of the country. I agree, but those bones
feel more like mine today, brittle and unforgiving.

Around Chambless, I fumble two discomfort pills into my
mouth, wash them down with cold bitter coffee. I find a half
of another in my pocket and I take that, too. I just want to get

us to Santa Monica, the end of the road. We've got less than two hundred and fifty miles now and hopefully John will be all right for five more hours.

After a while, the scenery starts to float. The sky has brush growing from it, but it doesn't obscure the sun any, which is high and hard now, blistering no mercy. I close my eyes, trying to shake off the dizziness. When I look into the sky again, this time I see an image of a glowing woman. I don't recognize her at first, but then it occurs to me that it's Our Lady of Guadalupe. Except that it doesn't exactly look like her. She's got a golden glow encircling her, like Our Lady, and a bright green shawl emblazoned with stars, but underneath it she's wearing a beige pantsuit, one that looks kind of familiar. She's also put on quite a bit of weight. In fact, Our Lady looks a lot like me, but younger. She smiles serenely at me, waves, then holds a finger over her mouth as if she has a secret to keep.

Still dizzy, I gulp the rest of the coffee that I've been holding in my hand for the past hour, hoping the caffeine will help keep me conscious. My hand smells acrid and smoky. I look at the cup and see grooves in the Styrofoam from my fingernails from where I've been clutching it. I look back up into the sky, but there's nothing but glare. I drop the cup on the floor of the van.

By the time we get to Ludlow, I feel better. I decide that it would just be best to forget what happened back there. I feel sleepy, so I crank down the window all the way. The wind noise increases and billows of warm air rush into the car, soothing at first, but seconds later it feels like I'm tumbling around in a clothes dryer, my head full of lint and bits of old laundered Kleenex. I roll the window back up leaving a crack of an inch and a half.

"What's wrong with the road?" John asks me. The heat rising from the pavement keeps tricking him into tapping on the brakes.

"John, it's nothing," I say, scared by the cars veering around us, the occupants yelling silently behind sealed windows.

Two minutes later, he asks me the same thing. Then again and again.

At Barstow, we stop for gas and at a McDonald's so John can eat. I suck on a small Coke to quell my nausea and clear my head. John finishes his two hamburgers, burps, and starts the van again as if he's been programmed to do so. We head back onto 66, but not really. The old road is buried beneath us, paved over by I-15. It's sad to think that they couldn't have just left it alone, but progress, that obstinate SOB, is adamant about such things.

The trees are different now. They are gnarled and knobby, corkscrewed into the earth, dark spines growing at the ends of hairy, welted branches that prick the air like giant bottle-brushes. They remind me of pictures of mutated cells that I've seen on TV. My book says they are Joshua trees, and since I've traveled this way before, you'd think I'd recognize them, but I don't.

Soon 66 rises to the surface again, but I decide that it's time for a shortcut. We stay on I-15, which takes us through the Cajon Pass, while bypassing San Bernardino, which I've heard is no great shakes.

Unfortunately, the drive downhill through the pass is very steep and wide and crowded. Six lanes of traffic, all going downhill too fast. Maybe San Berdoo wouldn't have been so bad after all. It's not long before gravity takes over and the Leisure Seeker starts going faster and faster down the precipitous incline.

"John," I say, watching the speedometer climb to 70 mph. "We're going kind of fast."

John ignores me.

Soon, we're doing seventy-five, then eighty. We haven't gone eighty at any point during this entire trip. The Leisure Seeker starts to vibrate.

"John," I say. "Please, John. *Slow down*."

What does John do? He gets in the left lane. We start flashing past cars on my side, each one whipping by like a gasp of unfinished breath. The vibration makes my head wobble. I clench my teeth, for fear of chipping my dentures. I'm getting really scared now. I see a sign up ahead:

RUNAWAY TRUCK RAMP

"John! Goddamn it!"

John says nothing. Eighty-five. Then something happens.

I stop being afraid. A calmness settles over me. I take a breath. My stomach feels better. The knot in my neck loosens and the discomfort eases. The draft at the window rises to a scream. Ninety mph. The undercarriage chatters like a tommy gun.

I close my eyes.

Then I hear a loud *thunk*. I feel the van slow down about 10 mph. I open my eyes and see John's hand on the transmission lever, as he slides it into L 2. Another, even louder *thunk* and a jolt as the van slows down even more. The vibration eases up as the engine of the Leisure Seeker howls, a spirit longing to be set free. I hear objects shift in the back as the speedometer slips down to sixty. John stares at the road straight ahead, grunts. He puts on his turn signal, moves over into the right lane. Someone honks at us.

I turn my head and look at the trees.

Quite suddenly, we are back on the old road. I am so happy to be off the freeway and out of the desert. I'm surprised at how nice Rancho Cucamonga is. (I think of the old Jack Benny routine—"Anaheim, Azusa, and Cuc-a-monga!") Here, Route 66 is called Foothill Boulevard and has been magically transformed into one long lush green strip of fancy shopping centers, restaurants, and office buildings. I have to say, it's good to see places that are thriving for a change. As we enter the town of Claremont, there is a sign:

LOS ANGELES COUNTY LIMITS

I am relieved, amazed, elated, and a little saddened to see this sign. It means we're about fifty miles from the ocean. I realize now that we need a plan. Everything I read about Los Angeles tells me that there will be nothing but traffic everywhere. I'm not sure afternoon is the time to venture into all that. I decide that we need a place to stay tonight. I direct John toward a filling station.

"Let's stop for gas, John. I need a pit stop."

I decide to let John take care of the van, while I grab the keys and wheel myself into the gas station. The bathroom is the usual indescribable mess. After I get myself put together, I head up to the counter. There's a middle-aged gal there, with frizzy brown hair, reading a copy of *US Weekly*. She's wearing a blue denim shirt with a Shell insignia on it.

"How are you today?" I ask.

"Oh, fair to partly cloudy," she says, giving me a smile.

I try not to stare at the spaces in her mouth where there should be teeth. "Would you happen to know of any good campgrounds around here?"

She scrunches up her face while she thinks. That's when I notice that Norma is also missing her eyebrows. There are just thin curved blue lines drawn where they should be. I wonder if she colors them to match her outfit.

"A few miles up Foothill you'll see a sign for a mobile home park. Turn there and it's just a little ways. It's a nice little place."

"Well, thank you so much."

"No problem, dear. You take care." Norma smiles again, wider now, unafraid to reveal what is no longer there.

Norma was right. The Foothill Boulevard Mobile Home Park is a lovely, clean little place, surrounded by trees, not too close to the strip malls. On the front door of the manager's office is a carved wooden sign that reads:

GOD BLESS OUR TRAILER HOME

Soon as we drive up, someone comes right to the window of the Leisure Seeker with a clipboard and sets us up for the night, just like that. As we idle through the park to our campsite, I get the feeling that these people have been living here for a long time. A couple of the trailers are painted cute colors like turquoise and dusty rose. Some have pocket gardens or flagpoles near the front door. One even has a little fountain with running water. It's a neighborhood. In short, I feel like we're home. At least as close as we're going to be.

"This is nice," says John.

It doesn't take us long to get things set up. After I have John pull out the canopy and put out the chairs in front, he disappears inside the van, closes the door behind him. I've hidden my purse, so there's nothing much he can get into there. I decide not to worry.

I should mention that I have formulated our plan. We're

going to stay here for a while. Of course, we'll go to Santa Monica tomorrow just to actually make it to the end of the road. That's important to me. We'll get up early to beat the traffic and conquer that last fifty miles. I want to see the ocean one more time. And by God, we're still heading to Disneyland.

I'm dozing in our sturdiest lawn chair in front of the van, when John opens the door, walks up next to me. I hear a familiar sound, a bubbly soft *pffft*.

"Hey, mister," I say, turning halfway. "Where did you find that beer?"

He stops, looks at the can in his hand and squints. "In the fridge."

"Would you get me one?"

"I'll split this with you."

"All right." I notice a triangle of foam on John's neck. I grab his arm and pull him down to where I can reach him. I wipe the foam off with my fingers. "What have you been up to? Did you shave?"

He feels his cheek. "Yep." He bends down over me and gives me a kiss, half on the cheek, half on the lips. It's as far as either of us can reach. I can smell Edge shaving gel and Old Spice aftershave.

"You smell good for a change, old man." I take another look at him. He's actually changed clothes, too. "What got into you? You're all duded up."

"Nothing," he says, like the senility has been a ruse, a really

234

good practical joke he's been playing on me for the past four years.

"Well, I approve." I don't know what brought this on, but every once in a while he gets a bug up his ass and actually does the things he's supposed to do.

John sits on the chair next to me. He hands me his can of Milwaukee's Best and I take a sip. It's so cold that it makes my eyes water. It must have been in the back of the fridge. I look over at him, clean shaven for the first time in days, no Sasquatch beard, wearing a decent plaid shirt and a pair of kelly green double knits that, if not clean, at least haven't been worn for the past four days straight. He looks like my husband again.

What's going on with this place? John's cleaned up, and I feel physically better than I have for the past two weeks. I don't know if it's because we're so close to our destination or what, but I feel healthy. I know it's an illusion, but for now, I'm enjoying it.

There isn't much left in the fridge so I decide that we have to go out for food. I don't know if I want to stop at a supermarket or a restaurant, but I'm actually feeling well enough to have a good meal and I want to take advantage of that. So we pack everything up again so we can drive. We leave our chairs and a few things sitting at our site.

There's nothing promising nearby. John wants to go to

McDonald's, but I nix it. Before we get too far, I just tell him to pull into a supermarket. We park in the handicapped space and luckily there's a shopping cart that someone left right nearby. I latch on to it and we head on in.

Ralph's Supermarket is big and bright and confusing. After roaming around, we finally find the beverage aisle. While John gets Pepsi, I lug a big jug of Carlo Rossi Dago Red into the cart and a six-pack of Hamm's. John might like another beer, I figure. After we pick up Cheez-Its and Wheat Thins, I feel myself getting exhausted, so I wheel us to the butcher counter and pick up a couple of nice-looking steaks, Italian bread, and twice-baked potatoes from the hot deli. On the way to the checkout, I find a few staples. Then we hightail it out of there before I keel over.

"I'm pooped," I say, once we get everything into the van, ourselves included. "Let's go home." Odd thing to say, considering that we're driving it.

I'll be damned, but as soon as we get back to the trailer park, I start to feel better again. I still feel like I could eat. So we cook up the steaks on the fry pan, warm the potatoes and bread, and pour ourselves a glass of wine. It's a wonderful dinner. For once, I eat almost everything on my plate. I feel full and content.

Afterward, we decide to watch slides. We do it simpler and safer this time. I have John set up the projector (which amazingly still works) on a card table by the door. I tape the sheet on the side of the van and we project up close. The images are about two feet by two feet. It's like watching television, except the show is your life.

Since we didn't go this time, we watch slides from a previous trip to the Grand Canyon, a long time ago. The first one is of me standing at the edge of the canyon. It's sunset, what John used to call "magic time." The whole canyon glows with a rich vermilion light. John was far away when he took this shot and since I'm dressed in orange you can really barely see me, but I know I'm there in the corner of the picture, ragged layers of stone blushing beneath me, a fiery silhouette dwarfed by that great yawn of the earth.

I remember perfectly the outfit that I'm wearing in the picture. It was really cute—slacks and a floral patterned blouse, both in a burnt sienna. Even John commented on it after he took the photo, how much I matched the interior of the canyon. "I'm one with nature," I remember saying. John laughed, but the kids didn't get it.

There's a whole series of canyon sunset shots. I push the button a little quicker with each one and create my own twilight. The colors grow deeper and darker—crimson gold burns into blood red—the canyon engorged. After five or six slides, I decide that the sun is taking too damn long to set. I click forward until we get to a daytime shot. The canyon looks entirely different.

With the bright morning sun bending over the craggy

rim of the pit, you can see all the different colors now, the rainbow qualities of the stone, the play of shadow upon shadow, the illusion of bottomlessness that is not bottom-lessness at all, but simply the Colorado River, doing its job, carving through eons of hard stone. I can see only a hint of the actual river in this shot and it makes me think that if this river can slice this deep into the earth over thousands of years, what's to stop it from just plain cutting the world in half? Could that happen?

I think about all that unstoppable water. My entire life would account for about one-sixty-fourth of an inch of this canyon. That's probably a generous estimate, I realize, but I find solace in this imaginary fact. Funny how sense of my complete and utter unimportance soothes me these days.

"That's a beautiful shot, John."

John yawns and says, "I'm going to go to bed."

I don't want to go in yet. It's a lovely night and I'm happy to be here with John. I hold out my glass for him to fill. "Just one more, John."

We watch one more half tray of slides, a trip we took to the Pacific Northwest. There are shots of us in a sweet little town called Victoria, just outside Vancouver in British Columbia. I loved that town. It was so clean and quaint and innocent. It doesn't look at all like where I grew up in Detroit on Tillman Street, but it looks like how the world looked then. Not so dangerous, so burdened, so sad.

The final slide is a nice one of John and I standing in front of a castle in Victoria, taken by our friends Dorothy and Al.

"That's the last one," I say, and before I can say anything else, John gets up and lifts the projector from the table.

"John," I yell. "For God's sake, let me turn it off."

He pays no attention to me. I follow the image of us as it zigzags like a flashlight beam, projected on the trailer next door, then across the road, then on the trees, then finally into the sky, where it is released completely, a mist of light.

"Put it *down,* John!" I say.

Sheepishly, John looks at me, then sets the projector back on the table.

My alarm goes off at 4:30. In the dim oven light above our kitchenette, I wrestle myself to my feet and find my way to the bathroom. Before I go in, I put on water for instant coffee for John and me, though I'm actually fairly awake. These days, I tend to wake with a start, heart clamoring at my breastbone. Even still, I take a breath and almost manage a smile. The cloudy mind and sandy eyes gladden me this morning for it truly feels like old times being up this early in the Leisure Seeker.

After the bathroom, I open the door to the van and peek outside. It still looks like night out there, but the darkness has a sepia quality that tells me it won't be long before first light. John coughs raggedly, then opens his eyes. He's still in his clothes from last night.

"John, get up," I say. "We've got to get going."

He coughs again. "Why?"

"Because we don't want to hit all the traffic going into Los Angeles, that's why."

He grunts and I think for a minute that he's going to give me a hard time, but he gets up. My husband has spent his life trying to avoid things like waiting in lines and being stuck in traffic. This is right up his alley.

By now the kettle is boiling. I mix up a mug of coffee and hand it to him.

At 5:15, John is in the driver's seat and I'm right next to him. As we leave the Foothill Boulevard Trailer Park, I tell myself that we will, with any luck, be back this evening. I hope we can get our same space.

San Dimas, Glendora, Azusa, Irwindale, Monrovia—all small, well-kept towns, one right after another. Foothill Boulevard keeps changing names and I have to keep looking in my guidebooks to make sure we're going in the right direction. One interesting thing that we do see is a hotel in Monrovia that, according to one of my books, has got a design that's part art deco and part Aztec and Mayan. I can honestly say I've never seen another building like it and I'm not sure I want to.

Just before Pasadena, the road changes to Colorado Boulevard and I'll be damned if traffic doesn't start picking up the moment we get into town, even this early in the day. Pasadena looks pretty in this low light, but I'm too busy fretting about what's ahead to enjoy the scenery. I try to relax and look around at the palm trees and the stores and the lovely old buildings. John is doing fine. He's not saying much but he's driving like a champ.

My guidebook leads us onto Arroyo Parkway, then the Pasadena Freeway, where we get off at Figueroa Street. We head west on Sunset Boulevard.

We are in the city of Los Angeles.

Despite what I said earlier about the dangers awaiting old people in big cities, I have to admit, I'm thrilled to be on Sunset Boulevard. Having heard of this street all my life, it's fun to be finally seeing it. Traffic's getting worse and there are lots of parts that look slummy, but this street feels exciting to me. I guess we're getting more courageous as this trip goes on. That or more stupid. Either way, we're here.

The sun is gleaming high and bright now. It's going to be a lovely day, I can tell. I see a pretty young woman in a very short skirt and halter-top, standing in front of a discount store, staring at the van.

"John," I say, "was that a hooker?"

Then I see another woman, this one older and tired looking, leaning against the window of an abandoned restaurant. I feel sorry for these women, about their choices, about what

241

they have to do just to live. The woman looks at us as we pass. I raise my hand. She looks the other way.

We're supposed to shift onto Santa Monica Boulevard, but Sunset is so interesting I don't want to get off. My map says that Sunset intersects with Santa Monica Boulevard a few miles up, so I decide that we can stay on a bit longer.

The signs keep changing languages—Spanish, Armenian, Japanese. We pass tiny shopping centers crammed with foreign restaurants. I see Hollywood dry cleaners and Hollywood pizza joints and Hollywood wig stores. We pass TV stations and radio stations and movie theaters and guitar stores and nicer restaurants. Meanwhile, traffic keeps getting worse, but I don't mind it because there's so much to look at.

At the corner of Sunset and Vine, I see a sign that makes my breath catch. "John, look! It's Schwab's drugstore. That's where Lana Turner was discovered."

John turns to me. "Boy, she was built like a brick shithouse."

"She was sitting at the counter when some Hollywood big shot saw her and decided to put her in the movies."

"Probably wanted to get into her pants," says John.

I laugh. "Yeah, you're probably right." I look for the drugstore, but don't see it anywhere. I guess only the sign is there now. We pass an old Cinerama domed theater, then a place called Crossroads of the World.

We're getting closer.

West Hollywood is very flashy. There are huge billboards up and down the street, most of them with pictures of women dressed a lot like the ones I saw walking the street. There are fancy hotels, expensive-looking restaurants, giant heroic statues of Kermit the Frog and Bullwinkle the Moose. I see nightclubs with names like "The Laugh Factory" and "The Body Shop," but these sure don't look like the factories or body shops we have in Detroit. I get the feeling that people in Hollywood like to make people think they're actually doing work for a living. I see a lot of limousines that must be taking people off to do that alleged work.

By the time we turn back onto Santa Monica Boulevard, traffic is bumper to bumper, and the discomfort starts to come on strong. I crush a little blue pill between my teeth and wash it down with coffee dregs.

Frustrated, John sits back in his captain's chair, breathes loudly through his nose. I watch him creep closer and closer to a convertible in front of us.

"Take it easy," I say. "We've just got a bit more to go." Out the window, I see a homey-looking little restaurant with green awnings called "Dan Tana's."

"That looks like a nice little place," I say to John. "Like Bill Knapp's."

He breathes loudly again, says nothing, looks ahead at the traffic. I glance up at a billboard and see an enormous picture of two half-naked men embracing and frolicking in the surf, with these words under it:

GAY CRUISES FROM $899!

We're in Hollywood, all right.

After a long boring stretch of malls, storefronts, and construction, we finally arrive in Santa Monica. It looks like a nice town, but we're not here to see the sights. We're here for one thing only—to get to the end of the road. As the street numbers get lower, I detect the clean salt smell of the ocean. Even mingled with the exhaust fumes, it clears my head and replaces my discomfort with a trill of excitement. Up ahead, a sign over the street reads:

OCEAN AVENUE

In front of us, there are palm trees and a park, and I can see straight through to the flickering luminous Pacific. Above it, the sky glows white and blue. It looks every bit as glorious as I thought it would.

"John. Look. There it is," I say, pointing ahead of us.

"There what is?"

"The ocean, dummy."

"I'll be damned. We made it."

I am amazed and pleased to hear that John has some understanding of what we've been doing. I thought he only knew that it was his job to drive. I reach over and put my hand on his arm. "Yes, we did. We made it."

"*Hot* damn," he says, scratching his head.

"You got us here, John. You did a good job, darling."

John looks at me with the widest smile I have seen on that face in years. It makes me wonder if I have been too tough on the old boy. I guess I don't tell him that he does a good job very often these days.

"Turn left here, John."

Along the avenue, the shoreline park gets wider and I notice hobos milling around, doing nothing in particular. Even with their perfect suntans, they seem out of place here at the ocean, so clean and endless.

A few blocks later, we are at the Santa Monica Pier. The sign looks like it does in all my books, like it's been the same for years, an old-fashioned arch with letters like from an old Fred Astaire movie.

SANTA MONICA
YACHT HARBOR
SPORT FISHING*BOATING
cafes

"Turn right here, John. And go slowly."

We pass under the sign and I feel my heart flutter and lighten. I was not sure we could do this, but we did. I'm proud of us. Up ahead is a yellow-and-purple Ferris wheel, the one they used in that movie *The Sting*, so I've heard. I decide that this would be a fitting ending to today's journey.

"Come on, John. We're going for a ride."

We find a place to park and John pulls out the You-Go for me. The walk is not too far. The sunshine, the ocean air, and the fact that there are people around somehow steadies my gait, straightens my back ever so slightly, sharpens my wits. Then again, maybe it's just the dope.

Luckily, the line is short. The carny at the Ferris wheel, an unkempt man who looks like he just finished a three-day bender, says he'll keep an eye on the You-Go while we go up. I don't really have any choice, so I believe him.

"Don't worry," he says. "It won't end up in a chop shop." He laughs and reveals brilliant white teeth that look too perfect to be real. I can smell sweat and cheap hooch oozing from his pores. His periwinkle qiana shirt is grimy around the neck. He gives both John and me a clammy mitt to hold on to as we stumble into our little two-seat bench. I wonder if he expects us to tip him.

"Have fun now, you two," he says, flashing those Hollywood choppers at us. "No necking."

He pulls a safety bar down. We are locked in.

As we slowly rise into the air, the Ferris wheel makes a *tat-tat-tat* noise that is vaguely disturbing to me, but apparently not to John. I look over and find him asleep.

"John," I say gently.

He tips his head back, opens his eyes wide, then closes them again and lowers his head. I let him sleep. I watch the palm trees as they lift and fall with the breeze. The water is moving just enough to make the reflection of the sun warp and ripple, creating inky ridges in the surface. We rise and rise. This height and all this open air would have terrified me not long ago, but not today. I am a daredevil today. I am Evel Knievel. I am that Intimidator fellow from the NASCAR. I look down and locate the Leisure Seeker in the parking lot.

All the sounds from the amusement park fade now. I hear only the wind and the creaking of the machinery that holds us here. I have my hair pulled into its little pygmy knot at the back, but there are loose strands whipping my face. The higher we go, the more the air pummels me, keeps me from taking a full breath. Just as I start to grow dizzy, it dies down.

I can see the back of the Santa Monica pier sign. I remember that the Pacific Ocean wasn't actually the official end of Route 66, that the original end was somewhere else in Santa Monica on Olympic Boulevard. The Santa Monica Pier was later accepted as the unofficial ending because it made sense to people for the road to end at the Pacific Ocean. I would have to say that I agree.

I take a long deep breath of clean ocean air as our box seat on the Ferris wheel reaches the tippy-top. It's just about then that John awakens from his nap.

He looks around and starts screaming.

Later, back in the van, on the freeway, on our way back to the trailer park, I can barely keep from panting from the discomfort, which is back in force. In fact, on a scale of one to ten, it's about a fourteen.

"Are we on I-10, John?"

"Sure."

I don't believe him. I frantically search for an interstate sign, even though I'm almost positive we're on the right freeway. I directed us there, after all. I think I'm frazzled from our little incident on the Ferris wheel, not to mention the wrenching discomfort.

Just before we have to slow down for yet another traffic jam, I spot a sign that says I-10 East. I would breathe a sigh of relief, but I don't seem to be able to.

Finally I inhale. Loudly. John turns and looks at me when he should be watching the traffic.

"What's wrong?" he says. "You got a stomachache?"

"Yes, I'm going to take some Tums." I open my purse and fish out two of my little blue pills. I should have taken two before, but I wanted to be at least fairly clearheaded when we finally reached our destination. I try to wash it down with a swig of flat Pepsi from a bottle I find under the seat, but the pills stick in my throat. Everything almost comes gushing up. I take another swig and somehow manage to get them down.

"That wasn't a Tums," says John.

"It's better than a Tum. Watch the road."

Great. Now he's paying attention.

It is only when I wake up that I realize that I've been sleeping at all. I'm feeling more comfortable now. I lift my head slightly to look over at John who is staring at the road in his very own trance. Traffic is backed up and we're going about 25 mph. I wonder how long I've been conked out, how far we've gone.

"Where are we?" I say, still groggy.

John says nothing. I look at a sign on the side of the freeway and realize that we are no longer on I-10 at all. We are on I-5, just approaching an exit for a town called Buena Park.

"How did we get on this road?"

"You said to get on it."

"I did not, John. I was asleep. Don't lie to me."

"Aw, shit." I don't know if he's swearing at the traffic up ahead or at me.

"Damn it, John." I choke down another sip of Pepsi and look at my map. When I locate I-5, I see that maybe he hasn't screwed up so badly. We are about to approach the exit for Anaheim. And though I had my heart set on staying back at the good trailer park, I see that this probably makes more sense. We were headed here, anyway.

"Get off at the next exit, John," I say, smiling at what I'm going to say next. "We're going to Disneyland."

Of course, we're not going to Disneyland *today*. I'll settle for finding us someplace to stay for the night. Which turns out to be surprisingly easy. Disneyland is located not far from the freeway and there are billboards everywhere for motels, camp-grounds, you name it. I choose one and we get off the freeway, as simple as that.

The Best Destination RV Park is only about three miles or so from Disneyland, but it's away from most of the congestion. Los Angeles was bad enough, but this area is everyone trying to get to one place. Us included.

As we check in (no curbside service here—I almost fall on my doped-up hind end getting out of the van), the woman in charge mentions that they do have shuttle service to Disney-land. That's for us.

After we find our space, I make sure John drives in so the back of our van is facing the back of our neighbor's RV. Then I sit at the picnic table and give him directions as he sets up camp.

This place is not as nice as the good trailer park in Clare-mont, but it's not bad. The only problem is that everywhere you look in this campground, there are kids running around like wild Indians. (I guess it's wild Native Americans these days.) This takes some getting used to.

After my inspection, I happen to look up to see that we are directly in the shadow of a giant two-lobed water tower with a deep roundish base, completely covered with polka dots. It is ugly beyond all my powers of description. Yet another closer look reveals the secret: its silhouette looks suspiciously like a certain cartoon mouse.

After John finishes, I get my You-Go and take a lap around the van to make sure everything's in order.

"Good job, John," I say.

"I want a beer," he says.

It's 3:20 in the afternoon. Late enough. "Okay, you've earned it."

John just stands there.

"Go get it," I say. "You're not crippled."

"Where do you keep it?"

"It's in the fridge. Where it always is."

John disappears into the van.

"Get me one, too," I yell after him. I think for a moment and realize that I've been saying "You're not crippled" all my life. My mother used to say it to me. Now we're at the point where we actually *are* crippled.

But I'm still not going to get John a beer.

It's dark now and the campground has quieted down. Before, you could tell that there were a lot of oversugared, overstimulated kids all worked up from a big day at Disneyland. (That's how my Kevin was when we took him. We had to dose him with Pepto-Bismol before he could sleep, poor thing.) They've all collapsed into bed by now, stomachs souring, churning up bad dreams of looming giant rodents.

After sandwiches (I force myself to eat to keep up my strength for tomorrow), we set up the projector next to the van for slides. Tonight's show is Disneyland 1966. It wasn't the last time we were there, but it was the best time. The kids were both young enough to think it was the most wonderful place on earth. And John and I were plenty young enough to go on rides and enjoy it all through our children's eyes.

The first shot is Main Street swarming with people, the castle in the background. In the foreground, I am standing there with Kevin and Cindy, holding both of their hands, all of us smiling our biggest smiles. I notice how nicely dressed we all are.

The entrance to Tomorrowland—flagpoles and a little cart selling ice creams. On one side is a pavilion with a gigantic atom on it, but my eye is drawn to the huge red-and-white rocket ship straight ahead. That must have looked so futuristic then. Now, even to these ancient eyes, it looks ridiculous and old-fashioned. I doubt if that's still there. Is there even still a Tomorrowland?

The next shot is of Goofy kneeling behind Kevin and Cindy and giving them both a squeeze. The kids are ecstatic, but I notice that Goofy's oversized hand is behind Kevin's head. Looks like he's about to give him a good smack.

"Is that a dog?" says John.

"Yeah, it's Goofy, John. The cartoon character."

"That's not Goofy," he says.

I give him a look. "*You're* goofy."

In a later slide, the kids are riding around on little flying saucers. This must be Tomorrowland still because I see a futuristic-looking house in the background—a big mushroom with windows.

Kevin and me in Frontierland, both wearing coonskin

caps. He's adorable. I, on the other hand, don't look so good. I'm put in mind of one of my less successful wigs.

The next shot is of John and Cindy. There aren't that many pictures of John in our vacation slides, so I must have taken it. Cindy looks darling, but John seems to be missing his head. He must have put that in there a long time ago for comic relief. Apparently, it still works. Next to me, John is laughing like a madman.

The last slide is Main Street at night, with the castle lit silver blue in the background. In the sky, fireworks are going off, cresting, cracking open the darkness, shooting long tendrils of colored light down to the buildings, way longer than I've ever seen for fireworks.

"I used an extralong exposure on that one," says John.

"You did?" I say, still surprised at what he just pulls out of his memory.

I linger on this slide. I study that blue castle and those fireworks and realize that this is the image I've had in my head of Disneyland for all these years. Just like the beginning of the *Wonderful World of Disney* TV show. Maybe that's why I wanted to head here this time. I know it's ridiculous, but part of me wants to think that the world after this one could look like that.

Like I said before, I stopped having notions about religion and heaven long ago—angels and harps and clouds and all that malarkey. Yet some silly, childish side of me still wants to believe in something like this. A gleaming world of energy and light, where nothing is quite the same color as it is on earth—everything bluer, greener, redder. Or maybe we just become the colors, that light spilling from the sky over the castle. Perhaps it would be somewhere we've already been, the place we were before we were born, so dying is simply a return. I guess if that were true, then somehow we'd remember it. Maybe that's what I'm doing with this whole trip—looking for somewhere that I remember, deep in some crevice of my soul. Who knows? Maybe *Disneyland* is heaven. Isn't that the damnedest, craziest thing you've ever heard? Must be the dope talking.

I sleep horribly this night, never actually sleeping, only dreaming. For all my remarks about the sugared-up children, I'm the one who ends up dreaming of mice. Hundreds of them, swarming me, nipping at me, pulling away pieces of me, leaving only areas where wads of stuffing and burlap are exposed on my body.

I wake again and again from my twilight sleep. That's another expression I got from my doctors. They were forever telling me that their procedures required that I be anesthetized into a "twilight sleep," a term so gentle and calm sounding that no one could possibly object. Yet I found that, for me, their lovely sunset slumber was always filled with terrors and nightmares.

Unfortunately, the mice are just tonight's selected short. The feature presentation stars a particular nursing home that

I know all too well, though John and I have visited many of them. This is part of your duty as an old person. You do it out of love and obligation, out of fondness for families and friends, out of lack of anything better to do. It is bleak entertainment, but it gets you ready for what's ahead.

The nursing home I dream of is a place where our friend Jim spent his final months. His wife, Dawn, had died the year before, then his kids put him there. Jim and Dawn were our best friends, so we had to go visit. Twice a month, we'd limp through those rank-smelling hallways to see him, but Jim didn't even recognize us. Us, John and Ella, fellow travelers, people he had camped with for the past twenty-two years. We weren't the people he wanted to see. He wanted to see Dawn. The staff would tell us that he did nothing but roll around in his wheelchair all day and call for his wife. "Dawn," he would say. "Dawn? Where are you?"

My dream is of the last time we visited Jim. It was always torture for John to see his friend that way, but this day it was worse than it had ever been. Jim couldn't even talk by this time, couldn't even call for Dawn. He sat there in his chair, drooling, chin resting on his chest. Every now and then, his lips moved as if he were speaking some silent language that only he could understand. When we tried to talk to him, he just looked up at us, reacting to the sound of our voices with an endless, unseeing stare.

After we left, John turned to me in the car and said what he always said to me after we visited Jim. "I will shoot myself before I end up like that." But this last time, he said something else as well. He took my hand and said, "Ella, promise me, *promise* me that you will never put me in a place like that."

I looked at my husband and promised him that one thing.

I open my eyes a little after six, finally giving up on sleep. This crushingly bright California morning, I am feeling so weak I can barely hold my head up.

John is snoring. During the night, he pulled an afghan over him and it almost covers his entire head. I check to see that he hasn't wet himself. He hasn't, but he's getting ripe again.

I try to pull myself up from bed and don't quite make it. I consider rolling out, but fear that I will roll right onto the floor. I remember that I've left one of my little blue pills in my sweatshirt pocket. So I plunge my hand into the folds of my clothes, sift through the balled-up Kleenexes, finally locating the pill at the bottom. After I gather as much saliva as I can in my mouth, which isn't much, I swallow it. This will either put me back to sleep or allow me to actually get out of bed, one or the other.

When I wake up at 8:30, the discomfort has mellowed. John is lying next to me with his eyes open, staring at the ceiling of the van. I can't tell if he's lucid.

"John? You awake?"

He doesn't say anything at first and I think for a horrible moment that he is dead and I'm alone.

"John?"

He turns and looks at me, matter-of-factly. "What?"

"I was just wondering if you were awake."

"I'm awake."

"Good. I don't want to be alone."

He puts his hand on the back of my head and strokes my head and neck. His hand feels wonderful, the way it used to feel, but different. I think it's because my hair is thin now. He used to do this all the time when we were younger, then I started wearing the wigs and he mostly stopped, except when we were home and by ourselves.

"You're not alone, sweetheart," he says.

"I don't want us to be apart, John."

"We won't be."

He looks around at the inside of the van. I think maybe he's going to ask if we're home, but he doesn't. Instead, he says, "This is a good old camper."

"Yes, it is," I say. There is a long time where we don't say anything, but John looks at me so tenderly that it helps me to forget all the bad things. It's a look that makes me feel that everything that's going to happen will be just fine.

I smile at him. "Your hair is sticking out like Bozo."

He smiles back at me, but I can see his eyes start to mist over, dissolving back into the gray. I start to talk faster, more than I can get out at once.

"Are you ready for Disneyland?" I say, more loudly than I mean to. "Remember, we're going today. It's going to be really fun, John."

I scare him a little, but I'm trying to pull him back to me. I don't want him to go away yet. I want him to understand.

"We are?" he says.

"*Yes,* John. This is the last leg of our vacation. It's been fun, hasn't it?"

He doesn't know what to say. He just nods along, caught up in something he doesn't really comprehend.

"It's been real good," he says.

I place my hands on John's face, my fingers over his lips. His cheeks are coarse with hair, but I don't care. I move my thumb over a bump on his lower lip.

"It's all been real good," I say.

"I'm glad we're going away," he says.

He's confused. I think he thinks we're heading out on vacation right now. I could correct him, but don't.

"Me, too" is what I say to him. "Me, too."

"Are you sure you're up to visiting the park today, ma'am?" says the young man driving our shuttle van.

I want to say, *No, goddamn it, I'm not at all up to it today, but I'm going anyway.* But what I say is, "Oh, I'm sure we'll manage."

"They have motorized wheelchairs you can drive around in, might make things easier."

"Really?" I say, curtly. "Well, I don't like wheelchairs. I don't think we'll need that."

He looks in the rearview mirror at me and my You-Go and doesn't say a thing.

Soon as we drive up to the place I see that he's right. Everything looks so much more spread out than twenty years ago. You know how when you visit a place from your childhood as an adult, everything looks so much smaller? Well, revisiting a place as an old person is the opposite. It all looks goddamned enormous.

Still, I am determined to do this. We have to take a tram just to get from the parking lot to the ticket office. I have a hell of a time just getting on the thing until some considerate young man gives us both a hand.

By the time we get to the ticket line, I'm already exhausted. We get the "One Day–One Park" tickets and they cost a fortune. I suppose it doesn't really matter at this point. I put it on the charge card along with everything else.

"Do you have any of those motorized wheelchairs?" I ask, now realizing that there's no way either of us will be able to get around this place, especially as weak as I'm feeling today.

"They might be all rented by now," says the unrelentingly cheery young woman at the ticket booth. "You'll need to talk to the cast member there. The wheelchair rentals are on the right, past the turnstiles."

"Rentals? I was told they were free."

"It's thirty dollars for the electric ones. With a twenty-dollar deposit."

"Je-*sus Christ*." I look at John and he just shrugs. I don't remember Disneyland being such a gyp joint.

As I stop to catch my breath, I glance upward to watch the monorail glide above us.

"Get a load of that! Gee whiz!" says John, pointing in the air, thrilled at the sight of the sleek orange-striped airtrain. The transformation is complete. He is a child again.

I watch the tail slither into the distance. It still feels to me like a vision of the future. Except now, it's a future that I'm too tired to imagine.

When we pass the turnstiles, I head on over to the rental stand with John in tow. He's already looking disoriented from all the activity.

"Are you here for an ECV?" the tidy young man says to me. I'm not so used to a southern accent coming from someone who looks Chinese.

"A what?" I say.

"An electronic convenience vehicle. An ECV. That's what we call these." He points to the two remaining scooters.

"I guess we are." I get out my charge card.

He gives me the fifth "Aren't you a cute decrepit old lady?" grin I've gotten since we arrived at Disneyland. They like to smile at you here while they stick their hand in your wallet.

"Come on, John," I say. "We're gonna drive around this joint."

John brightens at the word *drive*. "Can we get the van in here?"

"No, we're going to drive one of those." I point to the little blue scooters.

The young man explains the controls on the chairs. I am leery at first, but after a quick supervised spin around the room, I'm pretty sure I can handle it. John, as usual, warms right up to anything he can drive. In no time, he's scooting around like crazy.

"I don't want you to go far away from me, John," I say, stowing my purse in the front basket. "You hear me?"

No, he can't hear me because he's already taken off.

HERE YOU LEAVE TODAY
AND ENTER THE WORLD
OF YESTERDAY, TOMORROW
AND FANTASY

That's what the sign says as we pass beneath a bridge into the park. It's dim and crowded as we walk through, and it makes me glad we're on the scooters. We are stable on these buggies and can't get pushed over, a good feeling for a change. As we emerge on the other side, I am amazed to see that Disneyland hasn't changed much, although it's certainly more crowded than I remember, especially for 11:45 in the morning. I hate to think what this place is going to be like in four or five hours. We'll be long gone by then.

There are families everywhere, flocks of strollers, two and three abreast. I see a herd of what must be three hundred kids all wearing the same navy blue T-shirts. There are children running around, screaming bloody murder. As we tool down

Main Street U.S.A., I'm a little overwhelmed. An old horse-drawn streetcar passes by; behind it a flivver honks at us, a rude *ow-ooh-ga*. Behind me, I hear the clang of a steam locomotive, a brass band playing a Sousa march. People are yelling to the left of me. A group of seven or eight young kids come up quickly on my right side, laughing and screeching. I make sure my purse is secure in the basket. Suddenly, John has disappeared again. I look to my left, to my right, but I can't see him anywhere. I start to get a little frantic.

I don't know exactly what happens then, but when I finally look straight ahead, I see that I'm about to run right into a giant Winnie-the-Pooh, who has appeared out of nowhere. I panic and forget what to do to stop this thing.

"Watch out!" I yell at his furry orange back. At the very last second, he turns. I look into Winnie's mouth and see a flash of panic in the eyes of the person in the costume. I hear him say "Oh!" just before he jumps out of the way.

I finally release my death grip on the accelerator and the scooter stops on the spot. All I had to do was let go. I yell my apology to Winnie-the-Pooh. He waves, but inside that costume, he's probably giving me the finger.

John scoots up next to me, laughing. "You almost ran over that bear," he manages to croak out between guffaws.

"Just about gave me a heart attack," I say, starting to chuckle myself. I'm sure it was quite the sight.

Main Street U.S.A. is like an old town square. We scoot around for a while, looking at city hall, the movie theater, the penny arcade. We roll past a little café, half indoor and half out, where a man is playing old ragtime piano. We zip in and sit awhile. When a waitress approaches we tell her that we just want to sit a little and listen to the music. She says we have to order something, so we both get Cokes. The man at the piano plays "I Don't Know Why" and "California, Here I Come." It makes me wish we could have brought the kids and all the grandkids here, but considering nobody even wanted *us* to go on this vacation, I guess that probably wouldn't have happened.

We are outside "The Enchanted Tiki Room" when it happens. One minute I was in line, listening to the birds sing "In the Tiki, Tiki, Tiki, Tiki, Tiki Room," the next minute, I'm on the ground flanked by Disneyland paramedics and surrounded by onlookers. I have no idea what happened.

"Who are you?" I say to one of the young men, who's just put an awful-smelling inhalant under my nose.

"How do you feel?" he says to me.

"I feel a little woozy, that's all." I don't mention the screaming discomfort in my side where I must have fallen, or the fact that my entire body feels like a sack of potatoes that's fallen off the truck and rolled seven blocks.

"We're taking you to the hospital, ma'am," he says to me, all muscles and confidence and conked blond hair. He must be a weight lifter. His head is connected directly to his shoulders. I look for his neck, but it's nowhere to be found in his paramedic jumpsuit. He reminds me of Jack LaLanne, only bigger and stupider.

I have a gander at the other guy, an older black fellow on the heavy side. He says nothing. I turn back to Jack LaLanne.

"You're not taking me to the fucking hospital," I yell.

I hear a collective gasp around me. All these fine Disney citizens, indulging their morbid curiosity by rudely standing around watching the old cow passed out on her keister, are simply appalled by my language. I look up to see a gigantic Mickey Mouse. He ratchets his head around at the kids present, then holds his hands up over his giant mouse ears.

"We have to, ma'am. It's Disneyland protocol."

I pull my arm away from him. I try to sit up, but he holds me down. I don't put up much of a fight because everything discomforts so bad.

"I don't care what it is, I'm not going," I say. "I'm fine. I just got a little dizzy. I'm not used to these contraptions of yours." I don't see John anywhere. "Where's my husband?"

Jack LaLanne looks at me like, *she's going to be trouble.* And he's right. I'm not going to any hospital. I am done with hospitals.

"He's over by our ambulance," he finally says. "He seems disoriented. Does he have Alzheimer's, ma'am?"

"He has a little dementia," I say, one of my biggest fibs yet this trip. Saying John has a little dementia is like saying I have a little cancer.

I'm getting mad now, and I get even madder when I see someone come up with a stretcher. "I'm not getting on that goddamn thing!" I yell, not even knowing where I get the strength to scream like that. All the people around us look alarmed, but not as much as Jack and his pal.

I know once they have me on that, all is lost. They will take me to the hospital, and this trip will not have its proper close. I don't know where I pull it out from, but as soon as the words leave my mouth, I realize that they are ones I can hold on to.

"If you put me on that, I will sue Disneyland for a million dollars."

There's nothing like a look of fear on the face of a heavily muscled man.

"I will do it, so help me God, you put me on that thing." I cross my arms and try to keep from wincing. I narrow my eyes at him. "And it will be *your fault*."

Jack waves off the stretcher for the moment. "Ma'am, there's something wrong with you," he says, voice straining. "We need to find out what it is." I can see a hint of true concern reveal itself across his lantern jaw, but I don't care. I will play this hand to the end.

"I know what's wrong with me and I don't need to go to any hospital to find out. I'm fine. Just help me up, get me back on that cart, and we will get out of Disneyland. You won't have to bother with us ever again."

He's weighing his options now. He takes a breath, glances over at his partner, exchanges a look, then turns back to me. "We'll have to have you sign a complete release, saying that you refused all medical assistance."

"I don't care. I'll sign whatever you want. Just get us the hell out of here."

"Fine," says Jack LaLanne, brusquely. He's disgusted.

Of course he's disgusted. I won.

After the cab drops us off at the Leisure Seeker (a first if there ever was one), I take my very last two little blue pills, give John a Valium, and we both sleep for a long, long time. The discomfort nudges me every so often, so I drift in and out, dreaming of my children, of vacations we have taken together and of some that we haven't. I dream of Kevin, the sadness always present in his eyes, the sadness to come. I dream of Cynthia, how she will be the strong one, bearing whatever happens, just like she always has. They will be fine, my dream self tells me. They know that their mother and father have always loved them, that whatever happens at the end of a life does not represent the entire life.

When I awaken, the discomfort is still there, but a bit more tolerable. The alarm clock in the van reads 8:07 P.M. The place is stuffy and sick-sweet smelling. It doesn't take me long to re-alize that our little fridge has conked out.

It's dark in the van, so I decide to put on a light. I had the presence of mind when we went to bed to bring our battery-powered lantern. As I lean over to reach for it, I almost lose consciousness again. I sit and pant for a minute or so before I can reach the lamp. I wipe my forehead. I click it on and the bulb winks, then slowly shudders as a brownish dim barely illuminates the room. The batteries are going, but it is the perfect light level for my eyes. I lie back down, still winded, but less so now. My body has taken a surprising amount of abuse this trip, more than even I thought it could take, certainly more than my doctors could have suspected.

It was all worth it. This trip, despite all that has happened, was well worth it. I'm sorry if I worried the children, but I have spent all of my adult life worrying about them, so I'm just going to call it even.

Beside me, John's snoring is like the sound of ragged sheets being ripped. After every third or fourth snore, there is a long period where his breath seems to suspend itself. It is after one of these that he snorts so loudly that he wakes himself. John rouses and searches my face with his eyes. I don't think he quite recognizes me at the moment.

"Is this home?" he asks, his voice grainy with sleep.

I nod my head.

I check and see that he must have wet himself a little, but it does not upset me, not tonight. I decide that while I still have the strength, I will clean him up, change his underwear. Every mother's car accident rule. I unbuckle John's pants and attempt to yank them out from under him. For once, he cooperates and lifts his bottom. I pull his pants down, shorts and all, but even with him cooperating, they don't come off easily. I soon find out why. John has an erection like I haven't seen on him in many years.

"Well, look at you!" I say. "You old dog."

I'm still not sure he recognizes me, but he smiles at me, a smile I recognize.

I pull off his shoes, strip the pants off him, breathing through my mouth, trying not to look at his underpants for it would surely ruin what I'm feeling right now. I hide it all in a storage area near the foot of our bed. I take out his wallet and toss it onto the table. I turn off the lantern.

There is a catch in John's breath as I touch my hand to his penis, and I realize that I had forgotten that sound he makes. It makes me smile and pulls me away from this ancient faltering body of mine. I look at his eyes, dreamy half closed, but locked into mine. I wonder if this could possibly work, I think to myself.

Why not? I think. Why not?

The twinge of desire I felt days before when John touched me as he helped me into the trailer, I feel it again, only more so. I feel it through the pain, through the bruises on my body, through my shrugging flesh, my vast life scribbled upon it. I feel it through my nausea, through my will to die.

"Ella," John says to me as I continue to stroke him, the skin dryer now, his eyes clearer. "Ella."

I can't think of anything I would have wanted to hear more right now than my name. My husband looks at me, pulls himself up, moves toward me, over me.

This is something the body does not forget.

=====

When the pain awakens me again, it is 1:17 A.M. John is sleeping so hard from the other Valium I gave him, he is not even snoring. The rhythm of his breath seems almost random at this moment. The exhalations, when they come, are long and shallow, a *shhhhh,* as if he is lulling us to a place of quiet. There is something so sweetly familiar to all this, after a lifetime of making love to this man, that it almost stops me from getting up to do what I have to do.

I get up anyway.

The moon is high and full, and the interior of the Leisure Seeker is lit with an opalescent mist that highlights only the edges of things. As I stand, I grab the table to steady myself. I move carefully toward our little cardboard chest of drawers, my legs stiff, but not shaky. Surprising, considering the exercise they got tonight. From the chest, I gather a favorite terry-cloth nightgown for myself and a pair of clean underwear for John. I pull the gown over my head, settle the spongy, loose fabric over my hips and legs.

I just decide to leave John in his T-shirt, dingy as it is. I tug the underwear on over his legs, but don't quite get them over his bottom. As if cooperating unconsciously, he turns on his side toward me and I'm able to scoot them up far enough for decency's sake. I pull the covers over John to keep him warm, then I kiss his salty forehead, and say good night to my darling husband.

MICHAEL ZADOORIAN

For the moment, I gently rest my pillow over his left ear. He does not rouse from his sleep. I locate my purse and pluck the keys from a side pocket. I turn on the lantern, but it's even dimmer now, barely enough to guide me.

I open the side door of the van. Outside, the Best Destination RV Park is absolutely quiet. The night air is cool against my legs, against the dampness between them. I look up. Above, there are no stars, only clouds moving faster than I think I've ever seen them move, long silvery forms skating across blue-black sky, voided only by the colossal silhouette of the Mickey Mouse water tower. There is an acrid hint of marigold in the air.

Quietly, I click shut the door, close all the windows, and make my way to the driver's seat. I squeeze my eyes closed as I turn on the ignition of the Leisure Seeker. The initial growl of the engine is the part that I fear will wake John, but it doesn't. Before long, the idle steadies to a muted rumble. Hazy tendrils of exhaust enter the van.

I get up from the driver's seat and carefully maneuver myself back into the living area of the van, where the lantern is now glowing brown, a kind of antilight. I'm comfortable in this dimness. I am not sleepy yet, but I already feel more like John, unable to discern dream from reality.

While I still can, I shuffle through my purse for my ID, then place it on the table. I do the same with John's driver's license, then I get up from the bench, and go lie down next to him.

I am ready for bed.

Before long, I start to get drowsy. I feel as I do after a long night of sleeplessness—that moment when one is conscious, actually conscious, of being tugged into slumber. You sense yourself entering the realm of sleep, watch yourself lie down there, settle comfortably into nothingness. The crevice of light narrows as the bedroom door is closed.

What's different is that usually that moment of awareness is what awakens you again, pulls you back into consciousness, but not this time. I know now that we have found that place between dark and light, between waking and sleeping.

Our travels end here and, simply put, it's a relief. At this point, I do have to say that I am sorry for what this might do to the children, how it might look, but I've explained it all in a letter that will be opened after all this. Lawyers, it seems, are actually good for something. Arrangements have been made, affairs put in order. Hell, maybe we'll even get out of paying what I'm sure will be an outrageous Visa bill.

I know this all seems horrible and shocking and lurid, but I have to tell you, it really isn't. Long ago, John and I made up our own rules, crafted from the most mundane of things: mortgages, jobs, children, quarrels, ailments, routine, time, fear, pain, love, home. We built a life together and will happily do what comes after together. I say if love is what bonds us during our lives, why can't it still somehow bond us, keep us together after our deaths?

End on a high point, I say. This has been a great vacation. I really had a good time. Had we stayed home, it would have all gotten worse a lot sooner, believe you me. I would have suffered much, much more. I'd have been subjected to all the indignities that modern medicine has to offer and nothing would have changed. Eventually, I would be sent home to die. Then after, despite his wishes, John would be put into a nursing home. For him, there would be a final decline of a year or two or three, each worse than the other.

But then, that's the sad ending. One of us without the other. It's what would happen if I didn't end the story this way. It may be hard to believe, but this, right here? This is the happy ending, friend. What we all want, but never get.

This is not always what love means, but this is what it means for us today.

It is not your place to say.

Acknowledgments

Colossal gratitude and affection and respect to:

My wife, Rita Simmons, who helped me through the long quiet period, who gives me strength and knowledge, who still makes all this so much fun.

My sister, Susan Summerlee, for her love and support through all the tough stuff.

All my Detroit friends who read and helped and encouraged and listened to a lot of whining: Tim Teegarden, Keith McLenon, Jim Dudley, Brother Andrew Brown, Nick Marine (pompous chuckle), Donna McGuire, Buck(eye) Eric Weltner, Holly Sorscher, Jim Potter, Russ Taylor, Jeff Edwards, Dave Michalak, and Luis Resto.

Lynn Peril and Roz Lessing for helping to keep me sane. Dave Spala in T.C. for encouragement and never listening to me. Cindy, Bill, and Laura at C-E for good mom talk. DeAnn Ervin for always wanting to help. Tony Park for writerly foreign intrigue. John Roe for great photos despite the obvious liability. Randy Samuels for the straight dope. Michael Lloyd, Barry Burdiak, and Mark Mueller for always caring for the materfamilias.

My truly wonderful and talented agent, Sally van Haitsma, and the memory of her father, Ken van Haitsma. My editor, Jennifer Pooley, whose unflagging enthusiasm, endless devotion to this book, and exclamation points were a much-needed salve to this writer's spirit. My friend and teacher, Christopher Leland, a man who never stops helping his students.

Most of all, to the memory of my mother and father, Rose Mary and Norman Zadoorian. Their lives continue to be an inspiration to me.

Finally, to Route 66, the people and locales, real and imagined.

The road goes on forever.